"Chad, don't dri

"You need to grab the _____ on the floor."

"Are you kidding me?" Shaye exclaimed. "If you're driving, there's no way I'm going to take that baby out of his car seat. I couldn't live with myself if something happened to this little one."

"Those guys behind us, they have a gun. If they take a shot, the metal back there isn't thick enough to stop a bullet from penetrating and..." He didn't dare finish his sentence.

She unbuckled, turned around and reached back, then quickly unfastened the baby from the car seat. "Be careful, Chad. Please."

She lifted the baby over the back of the seat and encompassed him with her body, and crouched down on the floorboard in front of the passenger seat. She looked up and her eyes were filled with terror.

"It'll be okay, Shaye. Maybe I'm making a thing out of nothing. It's better to be cautious than wish I had asked you to do that after something bad had happened."

Acknowledgments

This series wouldn't have been feasible without a great team of people. It is impossible to name all the poor souls who have had to listen to me talk about books, writing, story ideas, plotting issues, editorial letters, procedural and logistic questions, and my general nonsense. That being said, there are some who have gone above and beyond the call of duty in the name of a good story.

To start, huge thanks go out to my agent, Jill Marsal, who regularly has to help me steer the ship, my amazing team at Harlequin, including but not limited to Denise Zaza and Connolly Bottum, and my friend with the acronyms who helps answer all my crazy questions (you know who you are).

None of this would be possible without you. Thank you.

PROTECTIVE OPERATION

Danica Winters

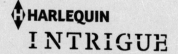

To those who serve in silence both at home and on the battlefield

Your sacrifices do not go unappreciated.

Your dedication makes the world a better place.

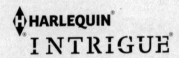

Recycling programs
for this product may
not exist in your area.

ISBN-13: 978-1-335-13565-0

Protective Operation

Copyright © 2020 by Danica Winters

For questions and comments about the quality of this book,
please contact us at CustomerService@Harlequin.com.

Harlequin Enterprises ULC
22 Adelaide St. West, 40th Floor
Toronto, Ontario M5H 4E3, Canada
www.Harlequin.com

Printed in U.S.A.

Danica Winters is a multiple-award-winning, bestselling author who writes books that grip readers with their ability to drive emotion through suspense and occasionally a touch of magic. When she's not working, she can be found in the wilds of Montana, testing her patience while she tries to hone her skills at various crafts—quilting, pottery and painting are not her areas of expertise. She believes the cup is neither half-full nor half-empty, but it better be filled with wine. Visit her website at danicawinters.net.

Books by Danica Winters

Harlequin Intrigue

Stealth

Hidden Truth
In His Sights
Her Assassin For Hire
Protective Operation

Mystery Christmas

Ms. Calculation
Mr. Serious
Mr. Taken
Ms. Demeanor

Smoke and Ashes
Dust Up with the Detective
Wild Montana

Visit the Author Profile page at Harlequin.com.

CAST OF CHARACTERS

Chad Martin—Chad has always been the one who brings joy and levity to any situation—that is, until his past comes back to haunt him in the form of a newborn baby, and thus his entire character is called into question. Soon they all learn that some secrets are far more twisted and surprising and assumptions are best left at the door.

Shaye Giest—Daughter of the crooked Algerian prime minister, Shaye has found herself becoming a victim of her father's wrath and mercurial temper. Just when things don't appear to be able to get any worse, she learns she has brought death to her savior's doorstep.

Wyatt Fitzgerald—The local sheriff's deputy, who quickly finds himself standing at the wrong end of a can of pepper spray.

Zoey Martin—Wild woman, tech genius, beautiful, smart, sexy and forever dangerous. Though she is constantly being challenged and tested by her family, she will do anything to keep those she loves safe.

STEALTH—The Martins' private contracting company, known for taking down those deemed unsavory by the US government and its many citizens.

Kash Calvert—The brother of Chad's ex-girlfriend and a man who solemnly believes Chad is the scum of the earth, no matter how much Chad tries to convince him otherwise.

Mindy Kohl—A socialite with a backbone and nerves of steel, Mindy is a woman not to be crossed. Teaming up with the Martins, they have created a new philanthropic-based line of tactical gear meant to keep the innocent safe.

Jarrod Martin—Chad's brother and Mindy's fiancée. Jarrod is ambivalent to the opinions of anyone besides those he cares about.

Trish Martin—Chad's twin sister, who was killed in action in Turkey while STEALTH was running an undercover operation in which they infiltrated terrorist organizations through the illicit gun trade.

Fenrisulfr Bayural—Enemy number one and the leader of the Bozkurtlar, or the Gray Wolves, a terrorist organization that works around the globe and leaves only murder and mayhem in their wake.

Chapter One

In a world filled with diamonds and pearls, Shaye Griest had never really thought about what she didn't have—the staff would take care of such things for her. She'd never found herself lacking tangible things. No, not when her father was the prime minister of Algeria, the head of state in the oil-and-gas-rich country. When she had been merely five years old, she had been given a gold-plated Rolls-Royce by the president of Nigeria with the flippant comment "for when you can drive."

Fifteen years later, the car sat in a garage in the underbelly of her father's lair in Algiers—where she would never see it, or her father, ever again.

Truth be told, she had never been a fan of the car, the man who had given it to her or her father who now held it in his keep. Good riddance.

She pulled up the collar of her coat around

her neck as she made her way to the Combine Diner in the heart of Mystery, Montana. The wind had started to kick up, making the bite of the December cold even more vicious. It was ten degrees outside, but it felt like she had stepped onto the dark side of the moon. She may as well be on the moon—her father would sooner look for her there than Mystery, Montana.

Or at least she hoped. The bastard always had a way of finding her.

The diner's wooden sign rattled as the wind pulled it against its chains, making a sound like the Ghost of Christmas Past. The sound echoed off the glittering snow that lined the edges of the road and sidewalks, reminding her of her abject loneliness.

She thought she had known frigid temperatures, thanks to all of her travels, but she had failed to calculate the level of desolation that came with the icy grip.

She should have run away to somewhere warmer; Tahiti was nice this time of year. And yet, the thought of Chad Martin and all he had done for her had pulled her in his direction.

She owed him and his family so much, yet instead of paying him back, here she was showing up in his last known location in a feeble attempt to find him, with nothing but her hat in her hands and a request for shelter. He and his family were hiding out and were probably long gone, but she had to try and catch him here. He was her only hope.

She should have texted before she flew to the middle of nowhere, but no.

A sane person would have texted, not dropped her family, been ostracized by her friends and then caught the next flight to a man who barely knew her.

What had she been thinking?

This was exactly the kind of pattern of actions and reactions her father had always criticized her for. She could hear his voice now. "Child, you will go nowhere, be no one. The weight of your imprudent decisions will always pin you down."

Well, damn it, she was going places and living her life as best she could—pins or no pins.

She walked to the door of the diner and grabbed the handle. It made a dull thump as she pulled against the bolt. The blue-and-red neon Open sign was glowing, its light casting a purple shadow on the snow. Apparently, *open* meant something different in Montana. Maybe it was more a suggestion of what could be if the conditions were just right…kind of like marriage.

The thought made the harsh taste of sadness rise in her mouth.

It had been nearly a year since Raj had been killed, but sometimes thoughts of his death struck her like a bolt of lightning.

She tried the door one more time, but it was just as locked as it had been before.

Ugh. She sighed.

The words *hot mess* clanked in tandem with the sounds of the sign's chains.

"If you're looking for a hot meal, you came to the wrong place," a man said from behind her, making her jump.

She reached into her purse and grabbed her pepper spray. She clicked open the safety, but didn't take it out as she turned to face the man.

"If you want food, Missoula is about twenty miles that way," the man said, jabbing his thumb toward a pink cloud of light pollution in the sky behind him. "And as safe as Mystery normally is, as of late, this ain't a real good place for a woman like you to be walkin' around alone."

The way he spoke was ambiguous. He was skirting the line between a threat and a warning. He was tall and lanky, and he stood with his feet apart and perched on his toes—the style of protectors. He must have been military, or perhaps law enforcement of some kind. Or maybe, just maybe, he was here as one of her father's minions.

It wouldn't surprise her if her father had someone posted at her heels.

He'd sent his people after her before.

She slowly pulled her hand from her purse, palming the pepper spray but keeping her finger on the trigger as she checked the direction of the wind.

It would send a clear message to her father if she took out his man.

"I'm not homeless, or needy. Thank you very much," she said, but as she spoke, she knew those words were a lie. She gripped the canister harder. "And if you are truly concerned for my safety, I think it best if you leave."

The man in front of her frowned and his hand slipped down to something at his waist. Before he could draw a gun, she pulled her pepper spray. It misted, throwing a cloud of capsaicin into the air. The yellow liquid hit him straight in the face and over his open palm as he tried to stop the spray from reaching his eyes.

"What the hell? No. Stop." He waved at her

as he was overtaken by a coughing fit. As he gagged and spat on the ground, he stepped toward her blindly.

"You can go back to whatever hole you crawled out of." She emptied the can, wishing she had bought something bigger instead of just the tiny one she had picked up at the gas station. Dropping the glittery can to the ground, she rushed toward the man who was gagging and spitting.

"Stop. Right. There," he said, dabbing his eyes frantically with the sleeve of his jacket.

She circled around him, careful to stay upwind from the spray. "Tell my father that I'm not his little plaything. I'm not coming home."

She had to get out of this one-horse town. If anyone knew she was here, and if her father was looking for her, then she would be putting Chad and his family in danger. Her father was capable of anything. In a different world, her father would have been the perfect hitman—he was cold, calculating and devoid of anything resembling remorse.

"Wait," the guy said as he staggered toward the pickup that was parked a few slots down from her car on the street. The truck was a banged-up old white Ford that had seen better days.

This hillbilly had another think coming if he thought she was going to listen to him.

She opened her car door, then paused and stared over at the staggering mess she had created. The man's eyes were red and puffy and tears streamed down his cheeks. But even as a slobbering, sweating mess, he wasn't bad-looking, even though he wasn't her type. And the ring on his finger was the nail in the coffin.

And he was no Chad.

As she stared at him, the man didn't even look in her direction—not that he really could—but something about his helplessness made her call into question whether or not he was truly one of her father's men. Her father usually employed only the best of the best, and this fumbling and spitting man was definitely not that.

A tiny bit of guilt wiggled up from her core. Maybe she'd been a little too defensive. Maybe she should have waited another second between seeing the threat and acting—but if Raj's death had taught her anything, it was that a single nanosecond was all it took to decide which way the sickle would fall.

The man grabbed a bottle of water from inside the cab of his truck and started flushing his eyes. As he worked, she glanced back at the ring on his finger—it was one of those newer black silicone ones and it appeared to be devoid of any normal wear and tear.

Most hitmen weren't married. It didn't fit the lifestyle—in fact, it was about as far from the lifestyle as a person could get. All of the henchmen she had ever met were made up of three things: muscle, too much testosterone and a machismo complex. But hitmen weren't all terrible. Chad Martin, for example, was built like a lumberjack—complete with the flannel shirt—with arms the size of small tree trunks, but when he spoke there was a hint of another kind of strength within him, as well. And it was likely that it was this charm and down-to-earth likability that made him even more efficient and deadly when pulling the trigger.

Damn it.

Even now, facing down a possible threat, she was haunted by Chad.

She got into her car and slammed her door shut. She shifted into Reverse and hit the gas without looking back.

There was a large thud as her car struck something.

She gasped as she stopped. "Holy. Crap."

Glancing in the rearview mirror, the man was lying on top of her trunk, facedown.

It was one thing to pepper-spray the man, but she hadn't meant to kill him. Oh, God, what if he was dead? And what would happen if someone had just witnessed her hitting him? What if she got arrested? How would it look if she did prison time for killing an American in the first days she was stateside?

Her father would have a diplomatic mess on his hands. And that was to say nothing about what she would do…or if she would even be able to walk away without prison time.

The blood rushed from her face and down into her toes as she stepped out of the car. "Are you okay? I'm so sorry."

He groaned.

Good. At least he is still alive.

Now to keep him that way.

She stepped closer and as she moved near, the breeze turned toward her and with it came the residue from her pepper spray. Her eyes started to water and her nose ran, and as she took another breath, trying to free herself from the spray, she only inhaled it further.

She gagged and laughed at what she had done to herself and to the poor man she had tried to take down.

"Laughing at me now, too?" the man said

with a groan. "You know, there are a lot of easier ways to kill a man."

She tried to open her eyes, but she could only squint, thanks to the pain.

"There's more water." She heard the sound of the man standing and moving toward her.

He kneeled down beside her and pushed a bottle into her hands. "Just pour it right on."

"I'm sorry," she said through wheezing breaths.

"Me, too." The man dropped down on the ground beside her as she opened the bottle and started pouring it over her face. The water was ice-cold, but it did little for her burning face and eyes. Instead, all it seemed to be doing was freezing to her eyelashes. "I didn't mean to scare you. I just thought with it being so cold and all, you might have needed a little help."

He wasn't helping the swell of guilt growing within her.

"This really is the backside of hell, isn't it?" she said, chuckling at where she had suddenly found herself.

"You ain't seen nothing yet," the man said. "If you want *real* cold, you should head up to the Hi-Line sometime."

"Hi-Line?" she asked.

"Clearly, you aren't from around here. The

arctic fronts run through there like a shiver running down the Devil's spine, freezing cows where they stand," the man said. He groaned as he tried to put weight on his leg, then he pulled up his pant leg. "Crap, there goes my dancing tonight."

Even through blurry eyes, she could make out the blood that twisted down his leg from a gash on his shin. "Seriously, I'm so sorry. I didn't see you back there. I just—"

"Wanted to get the hell out of Dodge," he said, finishing her sentence. "You're hardly the first person to step foot in this town and immediately want to head for the hills."

"That's not it… It's just—"

"I scared you…and you thought your father sent me," he said.

"Are you in the habit of always finishing other people's sentences?" she asked, slightly annoyed.

"Ha, it's sad, but you aren't the first woman to tell me that. My wife loves to constantly remind me." He rolled down his pant leg. "Now, what was all this nonsense about your father? Clearly, you're on the run—I'm assuming from him. But where you running to?"

Regardless of his ability to piece together the puzzle of her life, she wasn't sure she wanted to tell him anything. Considering the fact that she had pepper-sprayed and then nearly killed him, he was being remarkably nice.

He stared at her as she dumped the last bit of water on her face and gasped from the cold.

"You gonna tell me, or will I have to play twenty questions to get it out of you?" he persisted.

"Actually," she began, "I'm here looking for a man. His name is Chad Martin. Do you happen to know where I can find him?"

The man stood up, then reached behind his back and pulled out a set of handcuffs. Before she could even react, he had her arms behind her back and the cuffs flipped over her wrists. "Lady, I don't know who the hell you are or what the hell you are doing here, but if you're looking for Chad, you ain't gonna find nothing but trouble."

Chapter Two

Chad Martin looked around his cousin's barn. It was the quintessential guest-ranch barn, designed to charm their visitors. Everything hung from the wall in neat order. On each halter was a shiny little badge with a horse's name. On the top shelf of the tack room was an assortment of different-size helmets, and there were at least twice as many stalls as at the Martins' place, the Widow Maker Ranch. Ever since Gwen had sold the Widow Maker property to his family, it was almost a ghost town—they had a few pieces of necessary equipment and a saddle or two, but that was about it. They only had Sergeant, the black gelding, who was more of his sister's pasture ornament than anything else.

After Gwen sold them their ranch and moved in with her husband, she'd turned her sites to fixing up the Dunrovin Ranch. Atop the normal trappings of the barn, the ranch's crew had strewn up string after string of Christmas lights, wreaths, pine boughs and bows, making the place look like something from a Hallmark movie.

At the front of the barn they had set up a makeshift dance floor and the band was just setting up and plucking the strings as they tuned their instruments.

Though he had never been to a Yule Night Festival before, he was sure this was going to be one hell of a shindig.

His sister, Zoey, walked into the barn. Her hair was a bright red color that matched her Christmas gnome sweater. He laughed, glancing down at her gnome leggings as she walked toward him.

"Laugh it up, chuckles," she said, giving him a wink. In her arms was another sweater, which she thrust at him. "Guess what you're wearing."

He groaned. "No. I'm not wearing some ludicrous, ugly sweater."

"If we had a choice, do you think I would be wearing this marvel of modern fashion?" she asked, waving at her so-ugly-it's-cute outfit.

He chuckled as he unfurled the sweater, revealing a goofy reindeer with too-large eyes and a bit of hay sticking from its mouth.

"Wow, this is *something*. Please tell me this isn't one of the new bulletproof numbers you and Mindy have been working on."

She raised an eyebrow. "Come on now, you have to know that we have better taste than that." She smiled. "If our tactical-gear team came up with something like this, we would only use them as target practice."

"Are you telling me you want to use me as target practice?" he asked, teasing his sister.

"Just put it on before Mrs. Fitzgerald comes out here and sees you aren't dressed for tonight's event." She nudged him. "Their ranch depends on this night to cover most of their yearly overhead."

"Don't you think this is a bad idea?" he pressed. "We're in hiding, remember?"

"I've done the legwork, everyone attending has been cleared," Zoey said with an exacerbated sigh. "Dunrovin needs our help to make ends meet. Family does for family."

"Family or not, you do realize that if our CIA liaison saw me wearing this, I would be a laughingstock for decades." He slipped on the sweater over his T-shirt.

"You already are." Zoey stuck out her tongue, reminding him that even though she was team leader, she'd always be his older sister.

He snorted. "Where's Eli? Is he wearing something to match with you?"

"He was called to the Pentagon. For what, I don't know." Her face pinched. "But Jarrod is here and he has a gnome on his sweater. I'm not surprised you haven't seen him around. I'm sure he's hiding out in the ranch's main office, watching the game or something."

"There's a game on?" He perked up.

"Don't you even think about it," she said, wagging her finger at him. "You volunteered to help out as bartender tonight. Don't think you're getting out of it now."

"You better hope no one orders anything other than a Budweiser or they are going to be in trouble." He nudged his chin in the direction of the bar, which was set up in front of the barn under a heat lamp.

"I thought you might say something like that," she said, reaching into her back pocket and pulling out a bartender's guide. "Just remember, heavy-handed pouring makes for a short night."

"But bigger tips."

"If *we* were after the money, I could think of a thousand better ways to get it. To start, we could have let someone act on the contract that was out on you."

"*Was*. That ship has sailed, sister. Now, I'm

a free man." They both knew he was full of it. None of them were *free,* not with the Gray Wolves—the terrorist organization responsible for killing his twin sister, Trish—trying to hunt them down. But now wasn't the time to point out such nagging threats. Now was the time to put up their feet, take a little break from life and have some damn fun. For the last few months it had been nothing but a constant barrage of life's curveballs, all attempting to strike them out. For once, he wasn't going to let any drama ruin his fun.

He took the red book.

"Regardless," she said, passing over his little white lie, "we are here to help Dunrovin, not act like jerks. Don't make an idiot of yourself tonight. *You*, on your best behavior." Zoey pointed at him like he was still a five-year-old boy.

Zoey turned on her heel, then tore off to go after some other poor, unwitting soul.

As he made his way out of the barn and to the bar, he thought about the last time he'd really felt at ease—the days he'd spent with Shaye after they had gotten out of Spain. She had helped him find his center, thanks to the quiet days they had spent together in France, sitting at the wrought-iron bistro tables, listening to street performers and just staring out at the Mediterranean Sea. In a life as manic and dangerous as his had been for… well, *years*, it had been nice to breathe.

Though there were definite sparks, nothing had materialized between them. He had been there to avenge the death of her fiancé, who was also his best friend, not to make a move on Raj's widow. Chad took out his phone and scanned through the couple of photos he had taken of Shaye when they had been together.

Even though he shouldn't have been thinking about her, given who she was, he missed her. Hopefully she was doing okay.

He and Raj had met in the battlefield of Syria three years ago. Raj had come from a modest background, where hard work and determination were the name of the game and it had served him well in his work as a protective ops team member of STEALTH. He would do anything that was asked of him without needing micromanaging. He was like the unicorn of employees. Right up until he had fallen in love. After meeting Shaye, Raj told them he was leaving STEALTH and intended on going back to work for his father in the fishing industry—all so he could marry the woman of his dreams.

Chad had tried to convince him to stay, told him that no woman was worth giving up the good life—a life with no boundaries and a world just a keystroke away.

Shaye's father had hired a hitman to kill the man his daughter wanted to marry. Chad still found that unbelievable. And yet, from all he had learned, Raj had been aware of the danger. His friend had made a choice—one that had ended up costing him his life and Shaye her family and her childhood home.

However, after Raj died—and Chad met Shaye—he could finally understand why Raj had made such a crazy choice. Shaye had a way of smiling, with one corner of her lips, and the simple action made the world brighten around her. She was just like the sliver of moon on an otherwise dark night— her presence made those near her feel not quite so alone.

He slipped his phone back in his pocket as Mrs. Fitzgerald, the sweet and powerful matron of Dunrovin Ranch, came roaring through the front doors of the barn. Her gray hair was just a touch purple, but it was perfectly coiffed, and even as she breezed by him, not a single piece moved. "Places, everyone!" she called. "Our guests are beginning to arrive and the limos from the hotels will be here in just a few minutes." She fluffed up her hair as she spoke. "Don't forget to be kind, considerate, thoughtful! These are our friends, family and esteemed guests!"

Chad chuckled as he watched the nerves take over the normally steady woman. The way she lit up at the talk of the party and all her guests reminded him of Trish and how she had had always looked when they found out that they were being sent on a new mission.

It was almost the same look that she'd had on her face when they had gone to Turkey for the gun trade with the Gray Wolves.

The Gray Wolves... Trish...

Some of his joy slipped away at the memories of his twin sister.

He couldn't wait to say goodbye to this year, and all the heartbreak that had come with it.

He heard the sounds of chatter and laughter coming from the parking lot as a bus arrived with their first round of guests. Thank goodness they were here, so he no longer had to deal with the thoughts of all he had lost.

Some losses were too great to think about, too large, too all-encompassing and dangerous in their capacity to bring him to his knees. It was just so much easier to shove them away and lock them up in the area of his mind that he rarely allowed himself to wander.

Screw healing. Hopefully time would make him forget.

The first group breezed into the barn and a line formed at his bar. Most people were asking for spritzers, wine or beer—thankfully. But soon he found himself making up the night's signature drink—the drunk cowboy, his take on an old-fashioned. It quickly became a hit and the guests kept buying him shots in thanks.

A man sauntered up to the bar, an empty tumbler in his hand and a sneer on his lips. Chad recognized the man—he was an off-duty sheriff's deputy, Kash Calvert. "Oh, how the mighty have fallen."

Crap.

It had been years since he'd seen him, and time had done Kash no favors. He was only a few years older than Chad, but the crow's feet at the corners of his eyes and the gray at his temples made him look at least a decade older. For a split second, Chad wondered what had happened in this man's life that had aged him so prematurely.

On the other hand, the last time he had seen this man, Kash had been calling him a rotten son of a b—

Not that he hadn't had it coming.

"Kash, what can I get you?" he asked, hoping to get him moving along so he could stay out of his direct line of fire.

He thrust the tumbler at him. "Let's start with a drink, then we will go from there."

As Kash stared at him, a woman walked into the barn. Her dark hair was down, covering her face from his angle, but as she walked there was an air of breeding and plutocracy in the way her hips swayed from side to side, the action smooth and graceful but hinting at sexual prowess. It reminded him of Shaye and he went spiraling to thoughts of her as he poured the whiskey into Kash's drink.

He stopped pouring when the glass was three quarters of the way full.

Maybe the guy would take the heavy pour as an apology.

He splashed a bit of orange in the drink and handed it over. "This one's on the house."

Kash gave him a look of surprise as the next person in line pushed past him and gave his order. Kash started to say something, but stopped as Chad went to work. He was relieved as Kash turned and sucked away at Chad's best attempt to mollify him.

He worked quickly until the line finally dwindled and the band moved into full swing, playing old George Strait songs. As he wiped down his work space, he looked out at the dance floor. Shaye was standing there, her arms crossed over her chest and an expression on her face that made it clear she wished she was anywhere other than standing at the edge of a crowded dance floor in the middle of Montana.

He stopped wiping as he stared at her.

What was she doing here?

Maybe it was her doppelgänger. Shaye didn't know he lived anywhere near here. At least he didn't think she did. Was it possible that the Fates had brought them together at this place and this time, or was she here looking for him? The odds seemed long that she was still thinking about him, too, after all that had happened in Spain.

She was wearing a thick coat and black leggings, and stood out against the rest of the crowd, who were all wearing this season's best ugly sweaters—several complete with colorful Santa jokes. Maybe she was just like him and hesitated to participate in the nonsense, or maybe she wasn't here of her own volition. He knew all about that.

He closed down the bar for a moment, then walked across the barn toward Shaye as the band started to play "Honky Tonk Christmas." She glanced around at the two-stepping couples and suddenly looked about as comfortable as a ballerina at an MMA fight.

"Shaye?" he asked, rubbing his hands together in a feeble attempt to stave off his nerves as he walked toward her from across the room.

As she saw him, her eyes lit up and a smile took over her entire face. "Oh, my goodness, Chad!" she said, her voice taking on a high-pitched excited sound. "I'm so glad you are here."

Her eyes were red, as though she had been crying. "Are you okay? What's wrong?"

She rubbed at her wrists. "It's a long story and I may have been nearly arrested, but I'm here and I'm fine."

"Arrested? It must be a whopper."

"You have no idea." She gripped her hands in front of her, looking sheepishly up at him like she was about to ask for one helluva favor. "To be honest, I came here looking for you. You once said if I needed anything, you'd help."

"Absolutely," he said, surprised by her candor. Shaye had more connections than he and his family combined. If she was here, standing in front of him, asking for his help... Well, it could have meant any number of things, but first and foremost she must have been desperate. "What do you need me to do?"

If her request was that he was to kill a man, he was going to need an hour to finish his shift, then they could hit the road.

A look of discomfort washed over her features.

He glanced around at the crowd and saw a few people looking in their direction. "If you don't want to tell me here—"

He was cut off as Kash stumbled toward him, his empty tumbler in his hand. "Hey, man, you gonna get back to work or you just gonna hit on poor, defenseless women all night in hopes they'll take your sorry butt to bed?"

Heat rushed through his body and his cheeks felt as though they were on fire. He instantly regretted giving Kash the extra pour.

"Excuse me, I'll be right back," he said to Shaye, hoping to save himself at least a small amount of embarrassment—even if he had it coming.

He took Kash by the arm and made to move him, but Kash jerked out of his grip. "Come on now, *Chadie boy*," he said, spitting his name out like it was watermelon seeds. "What? You don't want to look bad in front of your new love interest? What is this, number five this week?"

Chad gritted his teeth as he attempted to check his anger. "Kash, if you want to take your anger out on me for what happened with your sister, then let's take this outside."

"Chad?" Shaye shot him a look as though she was trying to figure out if he was really guilty of the philandering the man was accusing him of or not.

"He is blowing a mistake out of proportion. Seriously, it's just a misunderstanding." He turned back to Kash. "Isn't that right, Kash?"

The man expanded like an angry puffer fish, and like the fish, his words were poisonous. Chad stepped back but Kash teetered toward him. "Is that what you call my sister—a *mistake*?"

Dating Kash's sister was a mistake, and he hadn't meant for anything to head to the bedroom, but Kayla had been lonely an emotional basket case. If he had been thinking straight, the nights they had spent together would have ended with a game of spades and a cup of coffee, but... "No. Kayla's a nice woman... I didn't want—"

Kash swung, his fist connecting with Chad's cheek. The pain was muted by the shots the patrons of the bar had bought him throughout the night. Until now, with the world spinning around him and the throbbing in his head, he hadn't realized how much he'd had to drink.

As he ran the back of his hand over his cheek, he stumbled. Kash was coming at him, his fist pulled back, and Chad watched as it came down upon him. Kash connected with his left cheek and he could feel the bones crack against each other. The dull thud of the hit reverberated through his skull.

He saw a swirl of stars as he felt his body hit the floor. A boot connected with his ribs as he crumpled into a fetal position.

As he struggled to remain conscious, he let the man deal his blows. No matter what physical damage this man did to him, it wouldn't hurt half as much as the pain in Chad's heart as he recalled all those he had done wrong.

He opened his eyes. Shaye stood a few feet away, watching in horror as the man delivered his beating.

Maybe that was why she was here—maybe she was his saving grace. Or maybe she was here to witness his final humiliation.

Chapter Three

She may have known how to make an entrance, but Chad sure knew how to make an exit.

Had he always been this much trouble?

Kneeling beside him on the floor, she pressed her fingers against his neck, checking for a pulse. His face was covered in blood and it streaked down his neck. When she finally felt the familiar thump of his heartbeat, she pulled back her fingers.

Not for the first time in the last few months, she found herself with blood on her hands. At least this time the sticky, hot blood was literal and not figurative.

She sucked in a harsh breath as she thought of Raj. She wasn't the cause of this fight between Chad and the man he had called Kash, but that didn't mean she wasn't to blame. It seemed like anytime she got close to someone, they always found themselves in trouble.

Chad mumbled something unintelligible

as she brushed the front of his hair out of a cut just above his eye.

"Chad?" she asked, the crowd around her starting to abate as everyone must have realized that he was still alive. "Are you okay? You need to wake up."

He needed to be okay. She couldn't stand seeing him hurt.

An older woman came hustling out of the crowd. She was well dressed, with a wide, muscular physique that spoke of years working on a ranch. She carried herself with a matronly air—this was her domain. The woman's hair was thoroughly hair-sprayed, but as she moved the wind caught an edge of it near her face and made a blade of hair fly up. For a moment, she could have sworn that the woman's silver hair looked like an axe just waiting to fall. And she had a sinking suspicion that Chad was the chicken at the woman's mercy.

"Get up, Chad," Shaye said out of the side of her mouth as she watched the woman descend upon them. At her heels was Chad's sister, Zoey.

Both women wore matching scowls.

She reached over and nudged him. Chad grumbled something and as he tried to speak there was a whisper of drink on his breath.

Looking to the crowd, she searched for a friendly face. All she spotted was Kash, sneering down at the man he had just left bloodied and battered—he would have to do.

"Kash, come here and give me a hand," Shaye said, motioning toward Chad.

"To hell with that," Kash scoffed.

"If you don't get down here, I will personally ensure that you spend the rest of your days cleaning latrines at an army training camp in Algiers, in the summer." It wasn't completely an idle threat. In the past her father had made similar threats and followed through on them. Though she didn't have her father's authority, it didn't mean she didn't still carry his confidence in administering justice.

Not that Chad was innocent.

No, her friend was far from that if he had done as Kash had said, but that hadn't given the man the right to dishonor her friend in a public place.

Kash stepped in and lifted Chad off the ground like a limp mannequin, just as Zoey and the older woman reached them through the crowd.

"What did Chad do?" Zoey asked, giving the older woman a side-eyed glance as she tried to hide her embarrassment. "Aunt Eloise, I'm so sorry about my brother and this scene he's created at your event. You know how he can be."

How he can be? What did that mean? From the time Shaye had spent with him, he had seemed like a good man. Sure, he had the culinary tastes of a five-year-old, loving macaroni and cheese and hot dogs, but that seemed to be his most glaring fault.

But now wasn't the time to ask Zoey for specifics about Chad's character.

"Does this have something to do with you?" Zoey asked, pointing at her.

She stepped back as if Zoey's finger was a dagger thrust straight toward her gut. "No. I—I just arrived. I have no idea—"

"Wait, *what* are you doing here?" Zoey asked, her eyes widening as she must have realized how out of place Shaye was. "Never mind," she said, once again turning her attention to the woman she'd called Aunt Eloise and the reddened state of her face. "I'll take care of this." She grabbed Chad's other arm and threw it over her shoulder.

Shaye wasn't exactly sure what she should do. She didn't really belong anywhere, especially not at this party, standing in front of its host, looking like she had caused a scene.

"Ms. Eloise, I offer you my most sincere

apologies," she said, with a slight supplicating bow. "It was not my intention for such events to occur."

Her frown disappeared as she looked at her. "None of this was your doing. Oh, I'm sorry," the woman said, extending her hand in welcome. "I believe we weren't introduced. And please just call me Eloise—Eloise Fitzgerald."

The woman's manners were the best she had found since she had come here, and they made her feel as if she was at one of her galas. She immediately took to the woman. She'd always liked a woman who was driven to lead instead of taking a back seat to a man—just another reason Shaye had to leave her father's control.

"It is a pleasure," Shaye said, taking the woman's hand in a demure shake. "I'm Shaye Griest, a friend of Chad and his family."

"Well, Ms. Griest, the honor is all mine. I'm glad you could attend tonight, and please pardon my nephew's manners. He was raised like a worm in the Big Apple."

"Thank you for having me. I must admit this day has turned out to be far more *interesting* than I had anticipated." She chuckled as she glanced over her shoulder and checked on Zoey as she and Kash dragged Chad from the barn. "If you don't mind, I must excuse myself. I want to make sure Chad is okay."

Eloise waved her away. "Why don't you all make yourselves right at home in the main house, all the guest rooms are booked for the night and there is no sense in you going anywhere."

This woman was full of surprises, and was nothing like the iron horse she seemed to be when she'd come steaming in.

Shaye hurried after Kash and Zoey, and caught up to them just as they were making their way into the parking lot.

Chad moaned, and his head flopped to the side. He looked as though he'd had too much to drink on top of the beating. Maybe that was part of it. Maybe he had been taking shots between pouring people drinks. From what she'd gleaned from his family, he could be the type. When they had been together, he had been so kind and caring, and he didn't seem like the man he was being portrayed as tonight.

Raj had always liked him. That had to say something, didn't it?

The thought of Raj made her belly do a little flop. Hopefully, if he was watching down upon her, he understood exactly why she was doing what she was doing.

"What should we do about him?" Kash grumbled.

It took a second for Shaye to realize they were talking about Chad and not Raj.

"Eloise said we would have to put him in one of the rooms of the main house—everything else is booked for the night." Shaye walked up beside Kash.

"If it was up to me, I'd drop him right here and be done with him," Kash grumbled. "He got what he had coming, and he knows it just as well as I do."

"Did he really?" Shaye asked, sounding far more naive than she would have liked.

Kash smirked. "I told you what he did. I ain't gonna repeat it." For a brief moment, he just looked at her, taking her in as he helped her friend. His gaze slid over her like a set of hands, but surprisingly it didn't make her uncomfortable. Actually, as she really looked at the man, he was someone she could have considered classically handsome, but in a Western way. He had Cary Grant features, with dark eyes and a pronounced jaw, and when he smiled—like he was doing right now—there was a single dimple that adorned his cheek.

If Shaye had to guess, this man could probably have any single woman at the party, and probably several of the married ones if he was so inclined. But perhaps he wasn't that type. He'd judged his sister and Chad harshly.

"I'm sure if Chad acted as you say he did, there was a reason. So be careful what you say—few things are ever as erroneous and detrimental as our presumptions about others." Shaye stepped closer to Zoey, who was studying them but staying quiet.

She didn't need Zoey presuming anything about her being there aside from her needing a safe place to land—which was in the *entire* Martin family's hands, and it was up to all of them if they would allow it.

And she certainly didn't need any man looking at her like Kash was doing right now.

Shaye cleared her throat. "We probably need to make sure Chad doesn't need a doctor. Don't you think, Zoey?"

"Uh, yeah," Zoey said, smirking at her as she glanced over at Kash. "Let's take him in, to the back bedroom. I don't think anyone is staying in there. We can check him over there. Kash, do you have your squad car or your truck tonight?"

Squad car? Was Kash a police officer? The idea caught her completely off-guard. It wasn't that she didn't think it possible of the drunk, surly, but well-built man, but it seemed strange that his revenge wasn't handled in a more *political* manner. If someone had acted against her father, they would have ended up dead in a matter of hours.

America was strange, but there was something to love about this Western, cowboy-style justice. At least all the things could be put on the table and dealt with in the open. Sure, it wasn't particularly civilized when blood dripped on the floor and they were forced to drag a man out of a party, but at least everyone knew where everyone else stood. And, to Kash's credit, he had picked up his enemy after the fight and was helping him—even if he was doing so begrudgingly.

Even Raj would have been more likely to kick dirt on his enemy instead of carrying him to his sick bed.

Maybe there was something to cowboys after all.

Yet, as handsome and drawling as Kash was, he paled in comparison to the enigmatic Chad. There was something about Chad that made her feel sorry for him. Well, not sorry exactly. She was more *curious*. Or perhaps it was mystifying. Chad wasn't like anyone she had ever known before. He was a mixture of all the things she found incredibly beguiling in a man. Whenever he was near, she found herself wanting to see more. But, for the most part, she could say the same thing about a car accident.

And, right now, getting involved any more than she already was would be the personal life equivalent of a four-car pileup.

As they made their way into the main house, she couldn't say she had ever been anywhere quite like it. It looked like something out of a John Wayne movie, with animal skins mounted on the walls and a roaring fireplace at the center of the room flanked by leather couches and chairs. A buffalo plaid quilt was folded neatly and hung over the back of the couch as though the entire room was just waiting for someone to come in and make themselves comfortable.

At the far side, standing tall, its gold angel touching the ceiling, was a Christmas tree decked out in white and gold, all except one bright pink Dora the Explorer ornament hanging at a little girl's eye level—the effect was breathtaking. Shaye peeked around her, half expecting to see a little one running down the hall that led to the room or laughing from inside the kitchen, which wasn't far from where they stood.

This was a home.

It was nothing like where she had grown up, where staffers constantly waited on her hand and foot. Sure, everything was spotless and in perfect order, but with that austerity came a certain distance—it was like the sterility of their palatial surroundings stripped the soul from the building and kept it from ever truly becoming a home. Compared to this place, Shaye had grown up in a museum.

Kash readjusted Chad, making him moan. "Can't we just dump him on the couch?" Kash asked.

Zoey shook her head. "You don't get to complain. You're the reason we're here. If you had half a brain, you'd have stopped at one punch."

Kash mumbled unintelligibly, but Shaye heard something about honor.

So even Zoey agreed Chad had this beating coming. She found herself shaking her head. This definitely was an entirely different world.

As they made their way down the hall, Chad started muttering as though he was coming back to his senses. "Do you think we should take him to the hospital, get him checked and make sure he doesn't have a concussion?" Shaye asked as she spotted the steadily growing lump on Chad's forehead.

"He doesn't have a concussion—he's just a drunk bastard," Kash growled.

Kash dropped Chad on the bed in the back room. His body was half off the mattress, but Kash didn't bother moving him as he left the room mumbling obscenities under his breath.

Zoey closed the door behind him and turned to Shaye. "Why are you here? Did you have something to do with this fight— with his drinking?"

Shaye tried to control her face, but she couldn't stop her jaw from dropping. Was that what Zoey really thought? That she had come here and immediately gotten Chad into trouble?

"No, I…" She panicked. "I had to get away from my father."

Zoey nodded and tried to roll the rest of Chad onto the bed. Shaye hurried over, grabbed hold of Chad's sweater and pushed the rest of him onto the bed. He was bent at an uncomfortable angle, but at least he was in one piece.

Zoey turned and there was a pinched look on her face. "But why are you *here*? I mean, I'm glad to see you. You know I like you, but we had no idea you were coming. And…as for how you found us…"

The blood drained from her face as she realized what Zoey was thinking. Zoey was probably concerned that she had managed to find this family in hiding. If she could find them, who else could?

"It's okay, Zoey. I didn't tell anyone where I was going. I only knew the town where I could find you because Chad once mentioned something about it. He knew I could keep it a secret. Don't worry," Shaye said, nearly stumbling over her words.

The worried expression on Zoey's face didn't lessen. "How did you find this party?"

Shaye couldn't help but bite at the corner of her mouth as she felt a new sense of shame. "Um, actually the deputy, Wyatt, brought me here after we had a bit of a *misunderstanding*." She thanked her lucky stars that she had been able to convince him that she had no intention of causing trouble for the Martins, and he had accepted her apology for accidentally pepper-spraying him.

Zoey scowled and seemed to study her for a moment before she finally relaxed. "And you are sure that none of your father's men followed you here?"

"My father and I are done. After he tried to kill Chad, and what he did to Raj, I'm no longer his daughter." The words felt like pebbles as they rolled over her tongue and slipped from her lips.

And that was to say nothing of how her

mother had died under mysterious circumstances when she was only nine. Her nanny
had told her that her mother had experienced
a heart attack, but had refused to answer any
further questions. When she was older, she
had heard whispers about her mother fil-
ing for divorce mere days before she died.
Looking back now, she realized that her father likely had a hand in her death…and its
cover-up.

The moment he lost control over someone,
they always ended up dead.

The only thing she had left from her
mother now was the ring she'd worn—a ring
that had been worn by her grandmother, and
now was stuffed in her bag.

She nibbled at her lip, as her thoughts
moved to the rest of her family, all of whom
had chosen to stand behind her father and left
her with nowhere to go—even though they
all knew what kind of man he really was.

"I don't blame you after all you've been
through. But I guess I didn't realize that you
and Chad…well, *you know*, that you were a
thing or whatever."

Shaye flushed. "Oh. No. That's not it.
We're just friends. He's like a brother to me.
He just told me that if I ever needed a place
to go that your door was open." Her body was

rigid as the awkwardness of the entire situation hobbled her. "I didn't mean to intrude, or bring any sort of danger into your lives. If you would like, I'm happy to leave."

Zoey paused for a moment, like she was thinking over their options. "No, you're fine. In fact, it will be nice having another woman around. Jarrod is here with Mindy, but they're in a honeymoon phase. And, well, Trevor is *Trevor* especially since Sabrina is away at Quantico in training."

"What about you and Eli? Chad told me that you two got engaged, as well?"

Zoey laughed, the sound high and filled with joy. "Yeah, I guess this getting-married thing is contagious. But, I gotta admit, I'm not in a huge hurry to pull on the white gown just yet. I'm loving this whole engaged thing. But I miss Eli. He's currently off the grid, but should be back before Christmas. At least I have this— Look at this thing." She flipped out her hand so Shaye could take a look at the rock on her finger. It was a beautiful ring with a sapphire at its center and around it was a ring of diamonds.

A wiggle of sadness and jealousy twisted through her. She had taken off the gold band that Raj had given her, but sometimes she could have sworn she still felt the weight of it on her finger. She missed the security of knowing that just like the circle of the ring, Raj's love was unending—that was, until his death.

A lump formed in her throat.

"You know," Zoey said, almost as if she could feel Shaye's sadness, "Chad is going to be all right on his own. Why don't you go back to the party and just enjoy the night?"

Shaye took a look over at Chad, who had started to snore. She should stay with him, take care of him throughout the night and ice his bruises. And yet, if she stayed here with him, she feared what could come of it. If he woke up and saw her taking care of him, the sexual tension that already pulsed between them would intensify. And if he asked her why she had stayed, she would have to tell him the truth—that she cared about him, that he was the only person she had wanted to run to and when she had been all alone, he was the man who had consumed her every thought. And it was this, all this *attraction*, that made it impossible. *They* couldn't be.

Chapter Four

One drink had been a mistake, but the sixth had been beyond absurd. Chad groaned as he rolled over in the bed and found his feet. He recalled Kash's fist, the sound it made when it crushed against his face and the copper taste of his blood mixing with the whiskey he'd been drinking before the fight.

And he remembered Shaye. Her turning and seeing him. The light in her face as she caught his eye. And the excitement he felt when he realized it was really her standing before him.

And then he had gone and made an absolute fool of himself.

He had to get to her. Explain what had really happened. Explain everything so he didn't look like a blithering, drunken idiot. He wasn't *that* guy. No, and hopefully Shaye knew it.

He stood up, but as he made his way to the

mirror, the world swayed and pitched under his feet. Drinking wasn't a solution, he knew. And he made a mental note to stop using it as a crutch—but damn, last night… Seeing Kash and Shaye. Watching the world bounce around him like it was nothing but a party… In the last year he'd lost his sister, gotten wrapped up in a kidnapping plot and seen more than his fair share of people die, even for his profession. And yet, people were out there dancing like it never happened.

It had been overwhelming—that level of oblivion.

If only he could go back in time and do things over. Raj would be alive, Trish would be alive and his family wouldn't be at the top of everyone's goddamn hit list.

They would go back to the shadows, doing a job where all they had to worry about was the task at hand and the targets that needed neutralizing—a world where they themselves weren't the targets.

He ran his hands over his face, and after doing a quick breath check, he found a trip to the restroom to be in order. As he walked in to the bathroom, he sniffed his shirt—it smelled like the barn mixed with the pungent sweetness of cheap liquor. Yeah, the schnapps at the end there had probably been the kicker he really hadn't needed. And yet, perhaps it was the elixir that had helped him take an uppercut to the face, one that had effectively ended his night.

He glanced around the foreign bathroom. There was a collection of toothbrushes in the stand by the sink. For a split second, he considered using one of them, but he stopped himself. This wasn't Camp You-Got-Nothing. Instead, he opened up the linen closet and extracted a new one that was still in the box.

As he caught sight of himself, he couldn't help but notice the welt on his cheek. Luckily, his eye wasn't too black and blue, but there was a faint purple line where Kash must have been wearing a ring. If nothing else, at least the guy packed a mediocre punch—if it had been someone else swinging, it was likely he would have found himself with a broken nose and a pair of raccoon eyes to match.

After a quick freshening up and brushing of his pearly whites, he stuffed his newly acquired purple toothbrush into his pocket. Aunt Eloise wouldn't mind him taking home a souvenir—it would be nice to have some daily reminder of the ass-kicking he had received. If nothing else, maybe it would help him make decisions that kept him between the lines.

He chuckled as he left the room. He and Trish used to always say that they needed to keep their lives like sandwiches—keep their asses between the mustard and the mayonnaise and out of trouble. Damn, he missed her.

He made his way toward the sound of voices wafting out of the kitchen along with the smoky scent of bacon. A woman was giggling, the sound so high that he wondered if it was the sound of someone truly enjoying themselves or if they were forcing themselves to laugh. Either way, the sound rang in his ears like empty cans dragged behind a beat-up car.

Tylenol. He needed Tylenol.

He opened the kitchen door and saw Shaye and Kash sitting at the antique wood table. He stopped and just stood there, unsure of how exactly he should proceed.

What in the hell had happened after he had left the party last night?

Shaye looked up at him and her face flushed. "Oh, hey. Good morning." She rushed to stand up and she made her way over to the frying pan, which was sizzling away on the stove. "We were just having eggs—want some?" She grabbed a plate out of the cupboard as if she had lived in the house for a million years, and not simply showed up on the doorstep last night.

"Uh, no." His stomach growled in protest of his refusal. "I—I was just going to get a cup of coffee and then head out."

Kash started to turn, like he was considering whether or not he wanted to face him, but he stopped. Instead he lifted his coffee cup in acknowledgment of all the things that could, should and likely wouldn't be said.

"Kash," Chad said, the man's name barely audible thanks to the embarrassment that weighed it down.

Shaye grabbed a travel mug and sloshed a bit of coffee on the counter as she poured.

At least he wasn't the only one who was nervous.

There was only one way to handle this situation.

He tried to think of something funny to say, but only one joke—the joke he'd learned for Anya, his niece who had Down syndrome—came to mind. "Why did the cowboy adopt a wiener dog?"

Shaye groaned, but he could see her relax as she handed him his cup. "Why?" she said, a smile peeking out on the corner of her lips.

"Because he wanted to *get a long little doggie*." He chuckled at his own inanity, and his feeble attempt to mollify the man whose sister he owed more than a simple apology.

Kash chuffed, but Chad didn't doubt that he was probably storing it away to tell his little cousins later.

Shaye arched an eyebrow and chuckled. "Seriously? That was awful."

"But I made you laugh. Job done." He tipped his head and made to leave the kitchen and the two of them. He didn't know what he had walked into this morning, but a few eggs and a cup of coffee wasn't enough for him to ignore his feeling of not being welcome.

"Wait," Shaye called after him.

She said something to Kash, but he couldn't quite make out her words from the other side of the door.

The door swung shut behind her as she made her way out to him. She grabbed her coat and purse, which were sitting beside the front door, then dangled a set of keys in front of him. "Zoey asked me to drive you home when you got up." She pointed to the parking area, where his white pickup sat waiting for them.

He ran his hands down the back of his neck and stretched out his chest, as if doing so would rid him of all the pent-up anxiety he was feeling. Unfortunately, it failed to do the trick.

He nodded, following her outside and getting into the truck without a word, though he had a bevy of questions about last night running through his mind. First and foremost, why were Shaye and Kash buddied up this morning?

And yet, he couldn't find an excuse that would give him a reason to ask her anything about it. He was already on thin ice, and he had no doubt that if he kept pressing her, Shaye would undoubtedly crack and he would lose having her in his life forever. It was best if they stuck together—they both needed a friend. He couldn't give her much, but he could give her a sense of safety if nothing else—it had been his job for a long time now, and it was the only thing he was half good at...*usually.*

He gave her directions as they made their way toward the Widow Maker Ranch. The nearer they got, the stronger the gnawing in his gut became. Though he had gotten out of Dunrovin with little fanfare and a crappy joke, he wasn't sure his family would forgive him quite so easily. Zoey was probably chomping at the bit to lay into him for making a scene. She had told him to keep himself in check, that they were there for the Fitzgeralds and to make it a seamless event.

He'd never been good at taking directions.

The snow had started to melt on the roads, and as they crested the hill that led to the house, the black gelding, Sergeant, greeted them with the throw of his head and a whinny he could hear even over the rattling of the truck's tired cylinders.

"Looks like someone is glad you are home," Shaye said, a tiny lilt to her words from her boarding-school upbringing.

"At least there is one," he said, half under his breath.

She gave him a look as though she was considering saying something to contradict him, but instead a muscle twitched in her cheek as she clenched her mouth shut.

What would she have said?

Unlike at Dunrovin, their house wasn't bustling with the sounds of morning when they walked in. Instead, they were met with the stench of overflowing garbage cans and dirty dishes. If Shaye was going to be here for any amount of time, he was going to have to get everyone on board with making more of an effort. Their life was a major contrast to her palatial estate. They really did need a housekeeper.

"You sure they said they were coming

home?" Chad asked, dumping the keys for the truck on the table near the door.

Shaye shrugged, then took off her coat and placed it over her purse on the table beside his keys.

Zoey's car was in the driveway, the tires free from snow or slush, so she hadn't gone anywhere lately. "Zoey?" he called, half hoping that she wouldn't answer.

It was quiet.

The back door slammed. Out of instinct, Chad put his finger up to his lips to shush Shaye and he moved in front of her. He could hear her breathing, faster than normal, behind him.

No harm could come to her. Not under his watch.

He tried to tell himself that the door slamming was only Zoey coming inside, but nothing felt right. He moved toward the back of the house and the kitchen. From just behind the door, he could hear the sounds of Zoey cursing and he relaxed; if she was sounding like a sailor, everything was fine. It was when Zoey was silent that he needed to worry. He stood up a bit straighter and cleared his throat.

"Is everything okay?" Shaye asked.

He sent her a comforting smile. "Yeah, it's

gonna be fine." He turned back. "Zoey, everything okay?"

She came storming out of the kitchen, her hair wrapped in a towel and her mascara running down her face. "So, you made it home? Good," she said, the words all nearly in the same breath. "The damn water heater went out. I went down to the mechanical room to see if I could figure the stupid thing out, and as wonderful as YouTube tutorials are… Yeah, we are going to have to call a plumber."

"You got something just there," Chad said, pointing to a blob of black streaking down under her left eye.

"Thank you, smarty-pants. I'm aware." She ran her hand under her eye, but instead of wiping it away it only made the inky mess worse, as she smeared it over her cheek and almost to her nose.

He bit his tongue. As fun as it was to harass his sister, the glare she was giving him right now said it wasn't time to tease—a cold shower had that effect on people.

"I'll go take a look at it, see what I can do," he said, though he was abundantly aware that plumbing wasn't exactly in his wheelhouse. "Shaye, do you mind hanging out with the banshee… I mean Zoey, while I go down in the crawl space and check things out?"

"No, that's fine," Shaye said, stepping over to Zoey. "And, hey, I think I have makeup remover." She got her purse as Chad headed to the mechanical room.

He could only imagine what Zoey and Shaye would talk about while he was out of earshot. He had a better chance of making it out unscathed from a battle with the broken water heater. Hopefully Zoey would set her straight about Kayla. After what had happened last night, no amount of apologies or insisting that it was all a misunderstanding would help him. People were going to think what they were going to think.

The heavy wooden door leading to the mechanical room had been swept clear of snow by the wind, and as he moved to lift the cellar-type door, it groaned loudly in protest, as though it wanted him there as little as he wanted to be there.

The wooden stairs creaked as he made his way down to the crawl space. The sump pump kicked on, sending a blast of mold-scented air in his direction. Of all the things that had failed, it was a wonder the sump pump hadn't gone first. With its black cast-iron parts and rusted joints, it looked like it belonged in the early 1900s rather than the current century. If they continued to live here, no doubt he would be back down here a hundred more times fooling around with all the things that could, and probably would, break down.

All the glories of homeownership.

The thought of domesticated life made his entire body clench. There was a lot to be said for being the kind who was always on the road. He definitely missed parts of his old life. Maybe, once things died down with Bayural and his henchmen within the Gray Wolves organization, he could go back to living out of a suitcase, taking assignments and getting reacquainted with his firearms. He looked down at his palms. The calluses he had built up over years spent at the firing range had started to diminish. With their disappearance came a surprising sadness.

He tried to shake off the feeling. Feelings were ludicrous. They were nonsensical, and rarely actually did any good. In his experience, feelings were a temporary problem that, if allowed to seep into his consciousness, always led to disaster. If he pushed them down, and just dealt with them on a need-by-need basis, he would be far more successful in keeping the disasters to a minimum.

And yet, here he was *feeling* all the things he really didn't want to feel.

On the topic of irrational fantasies, he had no idea what he was going to do about the situation with Shaye. On the one hand, he was so glad she was here so they could run away from their problems together, but at the same time her presence made him incredibly nervous. Whenever she was close to him, tension seemed to vibrate in the space between them. He wasn't quite sure what was causing it, or if he should even acknowledge the fleeting sensation. Maybe it was nothing more than his own mind playing tricks on him. If she was feeling in any way uncomfortable, no doubt she would've said something to him by now.

She wasn't the type who was going to sit by and be quiet about anything. When she felt that there were things that needed to be said, she definitely didn't hesitate to speak her mind.

She was a round peg in a square world. And he had always been a square peg in a round world, never taking things as seriously as he should have, or doing exactly what he had been ordered to.

The water heater was a silent sentinel standing at the center of the room. He opened up the side panel and peered inside. It was a collection of wires, circuit boards and thermostats. As he stared inside, footsteps moved on the floor above him. The women stopped walking, and as they shifted their weight, the floorboards creaked ever so slightly. As their movements stopped, he could make out the sound of his sister's voice.

"He's still hurting," Zoey said.

He didn't know if he should knock on the floor above him to let them know he could hear them talking, or if he should just shut up, listen and learn what his sister really thought about him.

"Aside from last night's performance, he's seemed okay around me," Shaye said. "In fact, he seems to be his normal joking self."

Zoey mumbled something and Shaye laughed—no doubt it was some comment on his character, but he didn't really mind. It was better to be laughed at and mocked than the target of everyone else's wrath. Being the family jester was far easier than being the family monolith.

"Losing Trish was hard on him. And I think being back here is making it a little harder on him," Zoey continued. "Being with you, and away from the family, he didn't have to face the loss every day."

"Do you think I should convince him to

leave? I'm sure he and I can disappear, be safe," Shaye said.

There was the creak of the floorboards as Zoey must have walked toward the kitchen sink. "One thing you will come to learn about our family is that we are fiercely loyal creatures. We aren't like most families, who scatter their children like seeds. We have learned, through entirely too much pain and loss, that when we are divided, we are at our weakest."

Chad inwardly groaned. Zoey needed to be quiet. Shaye was already hurting, she didn't need Zoey rubbing their strong family unit in her face…not when Shaye had just walked away from the family, the country and the people with whom she had spent most of her life. Zoey's words had to be a knife piercing Shaye's already shattered heart.

He grabbed a broom that was sitting by the door and moved to bang it on the ceiling of the mechanical room, but as he moved, Shaye spoke up.

"If you're worried about me taking him away from you, from this place, or from your team, you needn't be. I'm just offering him safe passage to wherever he needs to go, if he needs to seek refuge. I have no intention for anything more than that." Shaye paused and Chad lowered the broom. "Chad is a friend. A *good* friend. I won't deny it. But there is nothing else that could ever happen between us."

The broom slipped from his fingers and it clattered on the concrete floor, announcing his presence.

Zoey called down to him, quietly at first, but then louder.

He pretended not to hear, and instead slammed the metal panel shut and made his way out of the belly of the beast. Zoey had been right—he must be hurting. There was no other excuse for the way anger burst inside him at Shaye's words.

She didn't want him. That was fine. Better, even.

He stomped up the wooden steps and let the door boom shut behind him as he closed up the cellar. For once, he wished he hadn't stayed quiet.

Chapter Five

Ever since Chad had come back, he seemed to be in a sour mood. When Shaye caught him looking at her, he quickly looked away, and when she had asked him what was wrong, he had simply mumbled something and then disappeared into the back bedroom.

Not for the first time, Shaye questioned her choice in coming here. She tapped on her phone, looking for an Uber to take her to the airport, but the closest Uber was forty minutes away.

For now, she would stay put. Maybe call a taxi or get an airport shuttle.

She didn't know where she would go, or to whom, but anywhere had to be better than here. Chad had been a mess, emotionally and physically, since she had gotten here and she had a sinking feeling that his downward spiral was her fault. For both their sakes, she needed to go.

It was just… Well, she had thought he felt something for her. Especially when he had looked at her last night, when he'd first seen her across the room at the dance. All the distance that had been between them over the last few weeks had disappeared. He had been standing across the room from her, but it was as though they were pressed against each other. She had nearly been able to feel his breath on her skin and smell the sweet scent of his cologne and the heady aroma of his sweat.

But that feeling had been an illusion. He had made it clear with his actions last night that he wasn't the man she had thought him to be, and he was certainly not interested in her for anything more than a simple tryst.

If she wanted to get laid, she could have had any number of men. Sex and lust were easy to find, and truthfully she wanted neither. She wanted more. She wanted something like she had with Raj. She wanted to come home to her husband at night and find him happy to see her. She wanted someone to travel the world with, who had the same wanderlust that beckoned for them to keep moving, experiencing, finding adventures and perhaps a bit of trouble. She wanted to live with someone she loved, a man who could be her partner for life. Someone who wouldn't leave her bereft.

Not that Raj had wanted to die—no, he had died to be with her. And yet, he could have handled things so many other ways and instead he had pitted himself against her father, taunting him instead of playing the political games that could have kept him safe. He had known the risks, but he had refused to listen to her advice to make himself invaluable to her father. Things could have been different if he had listened to her; instead he stayed stuck in his ways. He had gone against her father after she had begged him to go along with him. In the end, he had been killed for his failings—but he had stayed true to who he really was.

She should have never let Raj into her heart. She should have known he wouldn't change to please her father. And if she had been smarter, she would have learned the same lesson sooner. If she had, perhaps she could have saved Raj. He had sacrificed himself by falling upon her father's contemptuous sword, all to stay true to who he really was.

If only she had been braver sooner.

Tears started to well in her eyes.

And here she was again, starting to feel

something for a man—a man her father had already deemed unworthy. If she stayed, if she allowed herself to feel anything beyond friendly for him, then she would be repeating her mistakes all over again.

She had to be brave.

Chad walked into the living room, slipping his leather wallet into his back pocket. The truck keys jingled in his hand. "I need to run into town, go to the hardware store and pick up some parts for the water heater. You want to go with me? If you're going to stay, I'm sure you're going to need a few things."

She glanced over at him and at the purple toothbrush still poking out of his pocket like a businessman's pen. "Actually, I forgot my toothbrush," she lied, as she tried to come up with any reason to be nearer to Chad.

Sure, she needed to be brave. She also needed to prove to herself that what she had said to Zoey was true—she didn't want anything more than a friendship with Chad. And besides, he could give her a ride to the airport. It couldn't be too far from the hardware store. And then she wouldn't simply run out on him.

Though, if she did run out on him, would he follow her?

Would he even care that she had left?

He probably wouldn't even bat an eye when she asked him to drop her off and would likely drive away as soon as her feet touched the curb.

How had she misread this situation so badly? All she had wanted was…well, to see *him*.

Mission accomplished. And failed.

Ugh.

It was painfully quiet as they rode toward the small town. The deeper he drove into the town, passing the late 1800s redbrick buildings with Western fronts and chipping and fading paintings on the sidewalls advertising long-gone pharmacies and bars, the more she started to wonder exactly where he was taking her.

She pulled her purse harder against her chest. If only he would just talk to her, tell her what he was thinking about, what he was feeling. She just needed some kind of sign for what she needed to do with the feelings in her heart.

She glanced out the window and watched as they passed by a hardware store. That had to be the shop he was looking for, but he hadn't even slowed down. "Hey," she said, motioning toward the store.

He looked over and slammed on the brakes. "Damn it."

Here she figured she was the only one who had been lost in thoughts of what could be, but there he was just as lost as her.

"Chad?" she said, his name barely a whisper.

"It's fine. I'm fine," Chad said, pulling into a parking spot right in front of the building. He slammed his hand against the steering wheel. "Actually, that's crap. I need to know why you really came here. Is it for me, or did you just need a place where your father couldn't reach you? If that's why you're here—"

"Chad, stop."

"I heard you talking to Zoey."

She gulped. "So that's why you've been in such a foul mood," she said. "Just so you know—"

"You don't need to recant what you told her. It's fine if you don't have feelings for me. It's probably easier that way."

Anger charged through her. Zoey had told her that he was hurting, and she was seeing it firsthand, but that didn't mean she didn't have her own feelings, too. "I'm sorry, Chad, that you overheard us and took it at face value. But please understand that there were things happening in that room that you may not have been privy to."

"Like what?" he asked, looking over at her with the raise of an eyebrow. In fact, he looked a slight bit hopeful, like somehow, somewhere deep within him, he wanted her to tell her that there was something more between them than just a simple friendship.

But she was probably misreading everything. And, even if she wasn't, she had already decided that it was best that she leave. This wasn't the right place for her. Nothing had gone the way she had imagined since the moment she had set foot in this stupid town.

"I think that maybe you and I…maybe neither of us really fit in the other's real lives." The words carried the sting of truth. "We are friends. We will always be friends. And, to be totally honest with you, I thought maybe we could have been something more. But I don't think we really know each other. You know?"

He tapped his fingers on the steering wheel. "You and I have a lot more in common than you think." He sighed. "What happened since you got here, it's not how things normally are with me. Kash… Well, Kash has me pegged wrong, and no matter how much

I want him to know the truth, sometimes not all truths are meant to be told."

Just like the fact that she still cared for him...no matter how poorly they fit.

"I get it," she said, looking into her bag. Lying on top of her pocketbook was a set of keys— Oh, her rental. How had she forgotten about the car? "Crap."

"What?"

She twisted her purse closed, afraid that if Chad saw the keys he might somehow figure out that she was planning on running away. It didn't make sense, all that she was feeling. Why did being around Chad always make her feel like she was totally out of control and that nothing made sense anymore?

With Raj, her feelings had been so much easier to understand...at least when they had first met. Things between them had been *uncomplicated*. And yet now, the only thing she seemed to have in spades was complications.

"Nothing," she said, faking a smile. "Why don't we run inside and grab the parts you need." She hurried out of the truck before Chad could say anything. Talking would only make her leaving that much more difficult. If she left now, at least she would do so knowing that it was the right thing, but if he said one more thing about truths, she would undoubtedly lose her nerve.

She glanced down the road, where she saw only a smattering of parked cars. Snow had started to drift down from the sky, reminding her of last night. So much had changed in such a little amount of time. A chain creaked in the breeze, and she caught sight of the same little wooden sign she had seen when she had arrived. Just a few feet away was her magenta rental car.

She could just send Chad inside and disappear.

There was a little bell as Chad opened the door to the hardware store. He stood waiting for her.

"You coming?" he asked. "You're gonna freeze out here." He pulled his jacket tighter around him.

It was the perfect weather to sit beside a warm fire, wrapped in a quilt, and sip hot cocoa with someone she loved. She glanced over at Chad.

Not that she loved him. Attracted to him? Definitely. *But love?*

Her body didn't shout *no*.

She hurried inside, brushing past him but careful to keep from touching him. As if touching him would weaken her resolve about leaving and the truths she was afraid of facing would bubble to the surface.

For now, they would worry about one simple water heater.

That was about as uncomplicated as life could get. Right?

She didn't even really know what a water heater looked like, but she was sure she had a better chance of fixing it than she did in setting things right with her life.

The hardware store smelled of grease and, oddly, popcorn. And aside from the elevator music playing from the sound system, the place was eerily quiet.

Was this what it was normally like, living in a small town?

A man came walking down the white-tiled aisle in front of her and gave her a nod. "Good morning, folks. Can I help you with anything?" he asked with a strong Canadian accent.

"Actually, we need some parts for our water heater," Chad said, standing beside her as he addressed the man. "Could you tell me what aisle we can find them?"

The guy led them toward the back of the store, asking questions about the model and what seemed to be the problem. It was a wonder that one person could know, or rather would want to know, so much about a single item in this store.

And then she felt like a jerk. Just because this man didn't have the weight of a country on his shoulders didn't mean that he didn't have passion for his job. In fact, maybe if she'd been more like him, with his clear love of all things tool-related, then maybe she wouldn't be in the position she was in now.

She chuckled as she thought about how her life was filled with tools, but not the same kind.

Chad's brow furrowed as he looked at her, and she stifled her laughter as she realized that it must seem as if she was laughing at the man.

"That is amazing," she said, as the man stopped walking and turned toward a long row of free-standing cylinder-shaped devices. On the other side of the aisle was what Shaye assumed were all the things necessary to install a water heater, including a menagerie of cords and doodads and a few different kinds of tubing.

Maybe she was wrong in thinking she could understand and fix water heaters better than she could her own life. Each had a thousand different options.

"I know, right?" the man continued, completely oblivious, or perhaps choosing to be oblivious, to her total lack of knowledge on the subject.

"We certainly do appreciate your time," Chad said.

"Don't be afraid to ask me if you need any more help. As you can see, it's pretty quiet in here." The man waved around the nearly empty store. As he dropped his hand, the bell rang as someone else made their way inside.

"Absolutely," Shaye said, equal parts nervous and relieved when the man headed down the aisle and toward the sound of the front bell. It was nice to have another person there, filling the silence that rose up again between them.

She felt a leave-it-alone attitude coming off Chad, different from the need to talk that had burst from him in the parking lot.

She walked across the aisle and ran her finger over the steel boxes. Their edges were razor-sharp and the metal was cold on her fingers, reminding her that this really was her life. She really was here.

Maybe what she needed more than anything was a minute to just *breathe*. She had been going nonstop ever since Raj's death. That had to be part of what was going on within her. This was nothing more than a bit of anxiety with everything that had changed in her life. Chad was her friend, and even if she was attracted to him, there couldn't be anything between them. Maybe he was right to clam up. If they talked about it, there was a large probability that it wouldn't end well.

Though she was tempted to run, maybe the best thing she could possibly do was just stay put for a week, at the very least a few days. Get some rest, and let her body recover from the stresses of travel before she started moving again. In the meantime, she and Chad… Well, maybe it was best just to leave that whole *idea* alone.

Or maybe she really should run.

"I have to admit," Chad began, "I have no idea what I'm looking at. Did you get anything that guy tried to explain to us?" he asked.

She laughed and some of her anxiety slipped away. "No, thank goodness you admitted it. I felt utterly daft for not understanding a single word that came out of his mouth."

Though they were only talking about water heaters, it felt good to get her mind off the swirling enigmatic torture she was putting herself through.

"I think I'm just gonna order a whole new water heater." Chad opened up his phone and pulled up a picture he must've taken. "It seems like this one is the same size." He pointed to a random tan-colored water heater, which to her eyes looked like every other one there.

"Do you think we need anything else to go with it?" she asked.

Chad tapped on his phone some more and stepped over beside her, pulling a random set of tubes off the wall. "According to YouTube and Google, I'm going to need one of these tubes." He lifted them like they were prize ribbons he had won for being the manliest man standing in the aisle.

"You know Google can be wrong sometimes, right?" she teased.

"Which is why I got corroboration on YouTube." He whirled the tubes around in the air victoriously.

She giggled at him. He was such a dork sometimes. Maybe that was one of the things she had missed most about him—his ability to walk into any snake pit of emotion and make a joke that changed the entire mood of the room. In fact, he was one of the few people she had ever met who had that ability. He could take her from raging bull to demure house cat in twenty words or less.

"Are you sure you grabbed the right size?"

she asked, raising an eyebrow at the number of different kinds of hoses and tubes that were still on the wall. "And what about like clamps and stuff?"

He huffed and grabbed a box of clamps from the wall, acting like he was almost doing her a favor by getting parts that she was sure he would need by the time this entire thing was over. She could see that they were going to be spending more than their fair share of time in this hardware store before he was done completely fixing what was broken.

"Hey, now," she said, holding up her hands in mock surrender, "if you don't think we need the hose clamps, be my guest and leave them behind. You don't have to do anything because I think it's a good idea." She could barely hold back her smile as she wondered how long he would go before he admitted that he had missed something.

He chuckled as though he was aware of the game she was trying to play with him. "We'll see if we need hose clamps or not. Really, I was just thinking about recycling. I'm sure that whatever parts we need are already on the water heater that's down there. Why replace good parts? I just care about the environment. Reduce, reuse, recycle—am I right?"

She rolled her eyes, the simple gesture making her feel like a teenager. But if he was going to act like a petulant teen, then she could, too. "Recycling, my ass." She laughed, the sound bouncing around the empty aisle like a rubber ball. "You and I both know that you need that part."

"Oh, you want to make a bet?"

"Okay, mister, but be prepared to lose." She crossed her arms over her chest. "What are you prepared to lose if you do end up needing those clamps?"

He tapped the box of metal clamps against his chin, making like he was thinking. He made a show of it, taking his time, but she had no doubt he had something in mind before he had even offered to make a deal. He was far too smart a man not to always have some kind of endgame.

"If I don't need the clamps, you have to—"

There was a loud thump, making her jump. "What was that?"

"Wait here." The playful edge left Chad's voice, instantly replaced by the cold sound of a trained member of a black-ops crew.

"No," she said, but as soon as she spoke, she realized how weak she sounded. "I should go get the salesman." She jabbed her thumb in the direction the man had disappeared.

Chad held up his fist, stopping her. He was already at the end of the aisle, clearing the area. Chad edged toward the front of the store. They were being jumpy, and as the song shifted to "Santa Baby," she felt even more neurotic because of their response.

Opening her mouth to say something to Chad, she stopped. He was nowhere in sight. She tried to laugh at herself, but as her body grew rigid, the sound came out as nothing more than a rasping wheeze. "Chad?" she called, her voice strangled.

There was no answer.

Had the Gray Wolves found them?

She started to rush in Chad's direction, but there was a loud *thwack* and pain screamed up from the back of her thighs as she plunged toward the ground. She turned and saw the two-by-four coming down, this time striking her in the calf as she tried to crawl away. Pain tore up her leg as the person hit her in the lower back, dropping her flat to the ground.

"Chad!" she screamed, covering her head with her arms.

She rolled to her right just as the board came cracking against the tile floor. The hit sent splinters careening at her face, one striking her just below her left eye.

There was the sound of footfalls as someone ran toward her. Chad. The box of clamps fell to the ground and the metal brackets skittered around her.

It was going to be okay.

She tried to move and stand up, but as she did, a fiery, brutal pain pinned her to the ground.

She rolled on her back, the action taking more strength than she thought she possessed.

Chad was standing at her feet, with his back turned to her. Pressed against him, with a black hose wrapped around his neck, was a man. She wiped away her tears. As they struggled, she caught a glimpse of the attacker's face. The long horse-face and bulbous nose belonged to someone she had never thought she would see again. A face she could never forget—it was her father's chief security officer.

She wanted to yell at Chad and tell him to stop as he pulled the hose tighter around the man's neck. There was a *pop* as the hose tightened against the man's esophagus. And, as the man struggled, he turned slightly and their eyes met. His face was red and sweaty, and his eyes bulged under the pressure of Chad's hold.

The man deserved to die. And yet, this could be their only opportunity to ask questions about her father and why he'd sent the man here. Did her father hire a hitman to kill her, just like he likely had killed her mother?

The thought sickened her. And yet, she had a sinking feeling that she was probably right.

"Chad," she said. "Don't kill him."

Chad's hold on the tubing remained the same. "He killed the guy working here. The poor man is lying over there by the front door with a knife in his chest. And you want me to not kill this guy?"

"I didn't say he doesn't deserve it." Shaye pushed herself up to a sitting position. As she moved, the fire from her thighs rattled up and she was forced to bite back a yelp of pain. The man certainly deserved to die, but they had to play this smart. "Chad…please."

She was tempted to tell Chad she knew the man. But if she did, what would Chad think? He would probably hate her for bringing more trouble to his life. What if he realized that she may have just brought all of his enemies straight to them because she had needed to be closer to him?

Even if she left now, her father knew about

the Martins—and likely knew about the contract Bayural had out on their heads. She had just put everyone at risk. No wonder everyone had seemed put out by her arrival. Maybe they had known exactly what a security breach she was.

Chad tightened his grip on the hose, and her father's man dropped to his knees, grasping at his throat.

"Who sent you?" Chad screamed, kicking him and loosening his grip so he could answer.

The man looked over at her and gave her a sickening grin. He reached downward and pulled a knife from an ankle sheath.

"Screw you," the man said, scrambling to his feet and jabbing the knife in Chad's direction.

Chad picked up the piece of lumber the man had dropped to the ground. "Put down the knife," he ordered.

"Give me the girl and no one has to get hurt," the man said, slashing the blade in her direction. "Shaye, do you even know what this man is dragging you into?"

What was he talking about? She jerked as she peered over at Chad. This wasn't the first time someone had hinted that he wasn't the man she had assumed he was. She needed the truth from him—the complete truth and not this whisking around it that he always seemed to do.

Chad looked over at her and then back to the man, like he was assessing for a split second whether or not he should do as the man commanded. "Tell me who sent you, and maybe I won't kill you."

The man laughed, the sound rattling off the metal shelving in the store. "Whether or not you kill me, it's not going to make a difference. Your family is going to die, but you shouldn't make this girl die with you, as well."

"Chad, don't listen to him." Shaye moved beside him, stumbling as she tried to walk. "My father sent this man. They must've been following me or something, but I doubt your family is really in any danger."

"You know this guy?" Chad asked, pointing at him with the beam of lumber.

She nodded, a foreboding sensation congealing within her. "He works for my father."

"I thought you said that you had split ways with your family. Didn't he know you were leaving?" Chad asked.

"I'm never going to be free of my father's grasp. I was foolish to think that he wouldn't have me followed." Or kill her…

But she couldn't tell Chad about her suspicions. She put her hand on Chad's shoulder. "Maybe it would be best if I go somewhere else. If I leave, at least you wouldn't have to worry about my familial drama making things harder for you and your family."

"You don't have to go back and be your father's prisoner. Not on my watch," Chad said. "If we kill this man right now, no one would be the wiser." He pointed up at the ceiling, where the white drop-down tiles were conspicuously missing any black, round eyes-in-the-sky cameras.

Just because they weren't being recorded didn't mean that someone in this little town wouldn't figure out that they had killed someone. And even if someone didn't figure it out, she would still know the truth.

On the other hand, this man had attacked her. If he'd been willing to harm her in order to do her father's bidding, what was going to stop him from killing her if they let him go?

"I am under direct orders to take you back to Algeria, no matter what." The man kept his knife raised, like a silvery rendition of her father's pointed finger. He would always be there, standing over her shoulder, commanding even if he wasn't present.

"You're only to take me back, nothing more?" she asked.

The man smiled again, his teeth stained dark brown, thanks to his many years of drinking black tea and smoking hand-rolled cigarettes. "As long as you behave yourself, everything should go fine."

"What does my father have planned for me upon my return?" she asked.

"Your father has plans, I'm sure." The man sneered at her, making chills run down her spine.

"Do you want to go back?" Chad asked with a sweet softness to his voice. He almost sounded like he was pleading, asking her to stay, without saying those words.

All of her wanted to stay with Chad. And yet, they were nothing more than friends.

If she stayed, things would only get more complicated.

She should've known. Nothing in their lives had ever been simple. No matter who was after them, or what evil was lurking.

She shook her head as she looked at Chad. "I don't trust him."

"Your father or this man?" Chad asked.

"Both."

Before she had the chance to tell him to stop, Chad swung the two-by-four, hitting the side of the man's head with a sickening thump. He hit the ground and blood oozed from the dent in his temple. Chad hit him again, this time a few inches to the right. There was a crunch, and she was sure his skull was fractured—likely beyond repair.

Part of her wanted to tell Chad to stop, and yet she knew that, given the right circumstances, this man would stop at nothing to kill her.

As Chad hit the man again and again, she finally reached over and touched his arm. "He's gone. And we need to go, too. If someone finds us here, we're going to go to jail."

He dropped the board and turned away from the man, but she noticed his hands were shaking. He had saved her life by taking another.

She would have to return the favor.

Chapter Six

She had already been through so much, and then this had to happen. Chad was glad he had killed the bastard.

As he drove, he looked over at her. She was pale and her hair was disheveled, but she didn't bother to right it and neither did he. Simply being shaken up wasn't even the start of it. From the way her face seemed to have momentarily aged and her eyes had darkened, she looked terrorized.

"Are you okay? Do I need to take you to the hospital? A hit like that to the back of the legs can cause clots, could move straight into your lungs. Dead in an instant."

Shut up, Chad, he told himself. *I need to work on making her feel better. Not worse. And seriously, telling her she could die? What in the actual hell is wrong with me?*

Shaye didn't answer, instead she turned her face away.

She thinks I'm stupid, too.

"I told Zoey that we are going to need a cleanup crew in the hardware store. She already sent someone out." He tried to sound reassuring, like he was talking about someone taking out the trash and not disposing of a dead body.

"You can't tell me that no one is going to report a murder. What about the guy who worked there?" she asked, her voice tired and drawn.

"He'll stay where he is. No one needs to know who the assailant was. We should be in the clear." He nodded like it was the perfect plan.

She finally looked his way and gave him a disbelieving look. "If I've learned any lesson, too well as of late, it's that nothing ever goes according to plan."

He couldn't help the chortle that escaped him. She had that right. "Yeah, but in this town, with my cousin as one of the few deputies, I think if we were forced to let him in on everything that was going on…well, Wyatt might see things our way."

"He may not entirely be on my side after what I did to him," she said with a guilty smile.

"Don't worry. I can get him to forgive you.

He's family," Chad said. But as he spoke, he wasn't entirely sure if Wyatt would come to their rescue or not.

"And what about Kash? He seemed hell-bent on revenge."

He twitched. He had forgotten about Kash. "Well, yeah, Deputy Calvert may be a bit of a hassle, but even he won't be able to trace this one back to us." He paused. "And besides, I think he has a bit of a thing for you. It may be our saving grace."

A hint of redness rose up in her cheeks. "He has no interest in me."

And yet, from the way her body responded to the sound of Kash's name and the mention of his potential interest, her naivety seemed dishonest.

Until now, he wasn't entirely sure what was going on between them, and unfortunately, he had gotten his answer. A strange sensation of jealousy penetrated his shell as he drove the truck toward Missoula.

"Where are we going?" she asked, her hand gripping the truck's door as if she was one step away from opening it, then tucking and rolling out onto the highway.

"It's okay," he said, reaching over and touching her thigh. "I just need to go and buy a water heater."

She seemed to relax under his touch, surprising him.

"There is no way in the world that I'm going to step another foot into a hardware store." Her hand slackened on the door. "I've already relived enough of *The Equalizer* to last me a lifetime."

He laughed out loud. "Okay, that was a good movie."

"A movie that I didn't think I was ever going to re-create in my actual life." She smirked.

"You have no idea. I was like one step away from grabbing a chainsaw and going all Denzel Washington on that guy's ass."

"Ha." She snorted. "Yeah right, *Denzel*. And, I have to say that if you moved here to have a quiet life, like he did in the movie, then you are failing miserably."

He shrugged. *Failure* was the word of the hour.

"I know, it's bad…" He laughed. "Over the last few months Zoey's been on me about reducing my kill-rate."

Shaye's mouth dropped open. "You have to be kidding me."

He laughed. "What if I'm not? What if the man you have befriended is the biggest badass ever?"

"Wow," she said, shaking her head at his complete nonsense. "Apparently adrenaline kicks your ego into high gear."

He flexed his arm. He wasn't exactly jacked right now, but there was a bit of burliness to his arms. Even if she wasn't completely impressed with his physique, he hoped he had her attention.

She laughed at him, the sound high and almost free of the tension that bounced between them in the car.

"Wow, you are the most ridiculous man I have ever met. Has anyone ever told you that?" she teased.

"I'll take that. I would much rather be ridiculous than anything else. At least I won't die of boredom anytime soon." He put his hand down on her leg and she moved slightly closer to him. "You know who might?"

"Hmm?"

"Kash Calvert," he said with a wry grin. "From what I hear, that man is about as much fun as a walrus on an iceberg."

She frowned. "A walrus on an iceberg? That's one I've never heard before. Is that really the best you can come up with?" she mocked.

"Hey, now," he said, glad she was feeling

good enough to tease him in retaliation. "I kick asses, I'm not a wordsmith."

Her sparkling laugh returned. "You didn't need to tell me that!"

He gave her knee a squeeze, silently thanking the Fates for the change in their moods. It felt so good moving back into the friendship that he knew was at the core of their relationship.

She reached into her purse, took out her phone and clicked on a few buttons.

"What are you doing?" he asked, trying to peek while keeping his eyes on the road.

She smiled. "I'm ordering a water heater and I just hired someone to install it. Hello, Home Depot." She hit another button with a flourish. "They'll be at your place tomorrow morning to handle everything."

He opened his mouth to protest. She couldn't have thought putting their address in connection with her name was a good idea. He gulped back his assumptions. "You didn't really just do that, did you?"

She frowned. "Come on now," she said, showing him the confirmation of their appointment on her phone. "It is a gift. And we both know you're going to need a professional, even with the internet's help." She stuffed her phone in her pocket. "And besides, if I'm staying at your place, I think getting your family a new water heater as a thank you is the least I can do."

Before he went into full panic mode, he took a breath. "Um, you didn't tell them to deliver it to our house, or give them our address, did you?"

She gave him a look like she wasn't following his logic. "How else are they going to do the install?"

"And you used your name and credit card number?" he asked, his voice a nervous growl.

She opened her mouth to speak, but then stopped and a tiny squeak escaped her. She threw her hands over her mouth and the color that had just returned to her features disappeared. "Oh."

He pulled his truck over to the side of the road and took out his phone. He dialed Zoey.

They had all agreed to stay at the ranch and face whatever came their way, but there was no way that they were going to survive this faux pas without a major fight. They had no choice—he and his family would have to leave the ranch.

"Oh, Chad, I'm so sorry." She spoke from the spaces between her fingers. "I wasn't thinking. I just thought I'd do something nice, and…" She choked on her tears as a few twisted down her cheek. "I… I'll cancel."

He waved her off. No matter what she did now, it didn't matter.

Zoey answered his call. "Another dead guy?"

"No. But we are going to have to hole up for a bit. Get everything you need out of the ranch house."

Zoey sighed. "What happened?"

"Nothing," he said, afraid that if he told Zoey about what Shaye had done that Zoey would take it out on her. "Our location may have been compromised. Is Anya there with Mindy?"

"Yeah," Zoey said. In the background he could hear her heavy footsteps, as though she was running through their house.

"Get them out—take them and Sarge over to Dunrovin. And you're going to need to pull our entire team to the ranch for backup."

The footfalls came to a stop, as though Zoey had stopped in order to think about the idea. "It will take a bit of work to pull them in from around the globe—and they're all working on contracts."

Their STEALTH team was currently strewn around the world, providing security for their clients. It was silly to think that using them for their personal security team was even an option. Sure, they could pull a few, but with so many people pointing in their direction now, that wasn't really an option. Their only choice was to leave.

Damn. He had really started to like living in one place for more than a month. Montana's state motto was The Last Best Place, which, for Chad, was the truth. The mountains that huddled around their small town and abutted the ranch were his fortress, his safety net.

He would miss this place.

"Send me the address of the new safe house," he said.

"For now, I'm thinking we stay in the valley," Zoey said. "It's a good defensible position."

The idea surprised him. Maybe she was as reluctant to leave their home as he was.

"You think that's the best option? You think you should talk to Jarrod first? You know, before we come up with a plan?"

He could almost hear Zoey bristle. "You don't worry about anything other than getting your butt home, and fast. Jarrod will go along with whatever I think is best. And right now, I think the best thing we can do is focus on our family, lure these bastards into one place and then strike down with the force of Thor's hammer. I want to be free of this weight. And the only way this is ever going to happen is if we kill them all."

He looked over to Shaye and thought about their conversation.

STEALTH was more than capable of cleaning up a dead guy here and there, but an entire menagerie of dead Turkish mercenaries and Algerian Special Forces was another story. And he wasn't sure he wanted to test Wyatt's familial bond or his willingness to sweep the Martin family's dirty deeds under the rug.

With the growing body count, he would need to work fast in order to protect not only the people he loved, but the town that offered them solace. No more innocents could die.

Chapter Seven

How could she make such an imprudent mistake? Shaye criticized herself the entire ride back to the ranch. She thought she was doing something nice, helping the family out, and instead she had made everything so much worse. Once again, she only had herself to blame.

Chad reached over and took her hand, like he could almost read her mind. "Don't worry about it, Shaye."

That was easy for him to say. All she could do was worry about her stupid mistakes and stupid decisions. Her entire life had been nothing but a mistake. If she didn't make it out alive, she had it coming.

And what if her father came here, looking for her?

"I can see you're beating yourself up, but you need to stop." Chad squeezed her hand. "Everyone makes mistakes, but you can't dwell on it. If we did, nothing would ever get done." His hand went slack on hers, as if he was thinking about all the mistakes he had made throughout his life—mistakes she wasn't sure she wanted to know about. Was he thinking about Kash's sister? More women like her?

His being secretive was both a comfort and a hindrance. She wanted to know him on a deeper level, but with that deeper level they would both have to unearth their skeletons.

And yet, with his hand on hers it was hard not to want more from him. He had just saved her. What had she done in return?

She groaned. "Tell me how I can make this right. I can leave." There had to be something they needed that she could provide, something other than the water heater and a spontaneous evacuation.

Based on her latest faux pas, he'd probably be smart if he told her to catch the next flight out.

He paused for a long moment, as though he was trying to think of something nontaxing and especially harmless that she could do to assuage her guilt.

He tapped on the steering wheel of the truck. "I know it's selfish, but I really enjoy having you around. With my siblings all coupled up, I sometimes feel like the odd duck." He glanced over at her as if he was gauging her reaction. "Not that we are a couple or, like, dating or anything, but well…if you don't have anywhere to go, it's nice to have a friend."

That wasn't the most romantic thing she had ever heard, but it still melted her heart. Truth be told, she was enjoying being around him just as much. It was nice to think about something besides her own family dynamics—even as her father's constant torment was still raining upon her.

"You're only saying that to be nice. I would totally understand if you thought it best if I left. From the moment I got here, I've brought nothing but misery and hardship." She touched her cheek lightly, motioning at the bruises on his face.

"Oh, you don't get to feel bad for these bruises," he said. "Are there any new ones? If there are, yeah, you can claim those." He sent her a wilting smile.

She laughed. "Well, I'm sorry about that guy trying to kick your butt back at the hardware store."

"As you should be." They rolled up to the ranch's parking lot, where Sarge was currently being loaded into the horse trailer.

She shouldn't have been surprised that this family would be quick to mobilize and would refuse to leave a man—or animal—behind.

Zoey stepped out of the horse trailer and latched the door behind her. Wiping her hands on her jeans, she made her way over to them. "We found a rental in the area, cash only, no names. It's about ten miles from here on the frontage road. We set up a series of cameras around here, so we can keep an eye on the place after we bug out. At least that way, we can see who our enemies are and act fast."

Shaye couldn't help but notice the way Zoey's gaze slid over to her.

"I'm sorry—" Shaye began.

"I'm sorry we were so slow in getting home. Roads are a mess, lots of snow," he interrupted, shooting her a look that told her she was to remain silent.

It only made her feel worse.

"I want you to stay and button up the last things after the rest of us leave." Zoey handed him a piece of paper. "Make sure nothing happens that could compromise us again when you come to our new place. I'll have new phones ready for you after you arrive." She motioned to the slip of paper, and gave

Shaye a look, not even bothering to hide her disdain.

Without thinking, Shaye stepped behind Chad like he could deflect the hatred in Zoey's eyes. The worst part was she couldn't blame her for being mad.

"I promise nothing," Chad said. "As the boots on the ground say, life sucks and whether you want to or not everyone has to take a ride in the blue canoe."

Zoey looked like she was trying to hold back a laugh. "Well, brother, we're not talking about just a few people who were impacted. Now, when we have to move out, we have Anya and our fiancées and the horse to think about."

"And whose fault is that?"

Zoey raised an eyebrow. "Really, Chad, are you going to begrudge any of us for finding happiness in our lives?" She nudged her chin in Shaye's direction. "Besides, we've had enough crap happen in our lives that it was about damn time for us to finally get a break."

According to Zoey's logic, Shaye should be getting her big break and finding happiness anytime now. And yet, with each passing minute, it was like happiness was drifting further and further out of her reach.

Chad reached behind his back and took hold of her hand. It was a simple action, and he had done it before, but this time it felt different. It wasn't just about comforting her. It felt protective and possessive, as though he would allow no one—not even his sister—to hurt her. Had something changed back there when they had come under attack?

She looked at the back of him. Before now, she had never noticed that he had a small brown birthmark at the base of his neck where it met the top of his shoulders. She could barely see it, as it was mostly covered by his jacket, and it made her wonder about all the other mysterious things he hid under his many layers.

"I'm sorry, Zoey," Chad said, finally taking a breath. His hand slackened slightly. "It's been a long day. And I appreciate everything you've done to pull this together. What all do you need us to do?"

Zoey nodded, seeming satisfied with her brother's attempt to mollify. "Just make sure that we leave nothing behind that can give us away. Then make sure the barn is locked up."

Chad nodded. They followed her over to her truck, where Sarge was stomping loudly in the horse trailer. Zoey got into the pickup. They watched as the caravan pulled out and Anya, Chad's niece, gave her a big, toothy smile and a joyous wave. Out of all of them, she was the only one who had a smile, as if her life was just becoming one bigger adventure and more wondrous things waited for them out there on the road.

She couldn't wait for a chance to get to know Anya better. So far, she'd only seen the girl in passing, and it hardly seemed like enough. Shaye had always loved children, but had rarely spent time with any. What little time she had spent with children had been like reliving her childhood. It was as if children had a magical power to, for at least a short amount of time, bring a sense of innocence to an otherwise burdened life.

She and Raj had talked about having children someday, but they hadn't had enough time together to make any sort of concrete plans. It was simply one of those things they had discussed superficially, almost as if they were talking about each other's favorite foods and not about bringing another human being into the world. How naive she had been.

Thinking back about Raj's favorite food, she couldn't even remember.

Just when she thought she couldn't feel any worse, his ghost came back to remind her of all she had lost—and, most importantly, time and memories that were slipping away.

If she wasn't careful, she would lose Raj entirely and be left with nothing more than a place in her heart reserved for the first man she had ever loved.

Maybe now she was doomed to live a lonely life as her penance for not being able to stop Raj from picking a fight with her father.

As they walked through the house, turning off lights and eating half a box of chocolate-chip cookies that someone had left on the kitchen counter, she and Chad barely spoke. It was like in the space between them, the echo of his sister's words circled—the family couldn't be compromised again.

Chad stuffed the last bite of chocolate-chip cookie into his mouth, and a crumb caught in the corner of his lips. She was tempted to reach up and brush it away, but she didn't trust her feelings enough to get that close to him. Right now, she couldn't trust anything she was feeling, least of all when it came to Chad.

"You've got something right there," she said, pointing at his mouth.

Of course, he wiped away at the opposite side, leaving behind the little stowaway. It made her laugh. He was so *normal* and she liked him even more for it. If she brainstormed about her ideal mate, *normal* wouldn't have been anywhere on her list— it would've been comprised of qualities like *ambition*, *self-motivation* and *a sense of humor*. But after getting to know Chad, *normal* was going on the list.

It was nice to see a man unburdened by the constraints of high society—he was free to be himself.

He wiped at the other side when she smiled and yet still missed the crumb, making her laugh out loud.

"If you're going to laugh at me, the least you can do is help a man out." He gave her a pouting look.

She stepped closer to him and brushed the crumb from his lip with her thumb. His lips were soft and warm, which made her wonder what it would be like to kiss those lips. They would be such a contrast to the strong, deadly man they belonged to.

Not that she could kiss him.

As she stood there thinking about him, she realized that her hand was still on his face, holding this unexpected moment longer than she had intended. And yet, she didn't pull away. Instead, she envisioned him pulling her into his arms and taking her lips with his in a moment of heated passion. It had been so long since somebody truly held her, kissed her, wanted her. She dropped her hand to his shoulder and he reached up and took it.

He placed his fingers between hers, only further reminding her of her carnal desire—the entangling of bodies and the heat of embrace. Her breathing quickened and a part of her she had nearly forgotten came to life.

Though she could think of a thousand reasons not to, she wanted him.

He moved in closer to her, his breath caressing her skin and she didn't have to wonder whether or not he was feeling the same way.

He reached around her with his free hand, wrapping his arm around her waist, drawing her closer to him. Their lips were mere millimeters apart, and she could've taken the helm and kissed him, but she held back. She wanted this stolen moment, and she wanted to know what it felt like to kiss his lips, but she also wanted him to make the first move.

She knew it was somewhat archaic, for a woman to yield her sexual power to a man, but in a moment like this, she wanted her lover to relieve her of her need to control.

"Have I ever told you how beautiful I think

you are?" he asked, the warmth of his words brushing like secrets over her skin.

She gave him a lust-drunk smile. "Keep talking."

He exhaled, long and hard, like he was releasing the pressure of being so near to her, so close to...

He kissed her. His lips were as soft and pliable as she had expected, but beneath their softness was a hard urgency, as if he needed to taste her...all of her.

Her body was electrified by his kiss, sparks of lust mixing with the flames of desire.

His kiss. Oh, his kiss. She put her arms around his neck, running her fingers through his soft, thick hair.

He roamed over her curves with his hands. Teasing her as his fingers slipped under the edges of her shirt, playing with the waist of her pants, making her body ache for all the places they could go.

Desire didn't even begin to describe what she felt for him—it was closer to a wild, unchecked primal *need* to be one with him, to be possessed by him, both body and soul.

"Chad," she whispered against his lips, wanting to draw him in even closer, but he leaned back.

Damn it.

She moved after him, hungry with the need to continue their kiss.

But the look on his face stopped her.

"Did you hear that?" he asked, suddenly on guard even though just milliseconds before he had seemed so vulnerable.

She strained to listen, but all she could hear was her own blood thundering throughout her body.

"Hmm?" she asked, the only word she could think of other than *more*.

"I think I hear a car outside," he said, but this time his words were slow, like he was somewhat legless after their kiss. "I bet Zoey forgot something."

She forced her body to move back from his. She'd already been castigated by Zoey, so she didn't need another browbeating.

If it wasn't for Zoey's arrival, Shaye had little doubt that things would have quickly escalated and they would've ended up making love right here on the kitchen floor, rolling in cookie crumbs.

The silliness of the cookies made her smile.

"You better go check on things," she said, smoothing her ruffled clothing and hair as though they really had made love. Zoey couldn't see anything that would give away their budding romance.

Not that she didn't already know that there were feelings between them. But hopefully she just assumed that it was merely friendship and nothing more. Their changing friendship didn't need a witness, at least not now. Not when things were so new and fresh between them.

He pulled down, straightening his shirt and cleared his throat. And as he turned away from her, she could see his body had been reacting in nearly the same way as hers.

She rubbed the back of her neck, about to comment, but then again she was sure that he was aware of his body's current state.

A sense of accomplishment filled her, though she knew it was somewhat ridiculous. But it had felt good to turn him on. She still had *it*.

She followed him out of the kitchen and toward the front door as Chad took his time, no doubt trying to right his state of affairs.

As they drew nearer to the door, they heard the sound of a car careening from the house. Outside, a gray Ford Escape was slipping and sliding as the driver, a woman, must have been slamming on the gas pedal hoping for a speedy retreat.

"That's not Zoey," she said, chastising herself for stating the obvious. Of course, they both knew that it wasn't Zoey. "You have any idea who it is?"

He shook his head, and there was a puckered expression on his face.

"You don't think it's somebody looking for us, do you?" she asked, fully back in their current reality.

It had been foolish to think they could steal a moment and kiss.

She had Chad, and if they were smart, they would make it out of this mostly unscathed. And if she had her way, maybe things between them could continue to progress.

Although, she wasn't entirely sure she was ready for anything more than a love affair. Anything else was far too dangerous for her heart.

The expression "dancing too close to the flames" came to her mind, but she pushed away the thought.

Chad stepped to the front door, moving like he was going to take off after the car. As he opened the door, he stopped. From where he was standing, she couldn't tell what he was looking at, but she could hear a long line of expletives.

"What is it?" she asked, hoping against

all hopes that whoever had come hadn't left them with any sort of explosive surprise.

"I... You—you aren't going to believe this." He let the door move farther open as he squatted down to something on the porch.

Oh, please be a puppy, she silently pleaded, though she was more than aware that the odds of her wish coming true were slim to none.

She stepped over to him and stopped. There, sitting just outside the door, fast asleep in a black car seat, was a baby.

"Oh," she said, the wind nearly knocked out of her.

What in the actual hell was a baby doing sitting on their doorstep? Who would have done such a thing? Why?

Her world spun out of control as she tried to fit together the pieces of a puzzle that had no edges. Apparently, nothing was outside of the realm of possibility when it came to this family.

"Whose baby is it?" she asked.

"I have no clue." Chad lifted the baby inside, closing the door as he brought the bundle over to the warmth near the dwindling fire.

"Does one of your brothers have a baby?" she asked, hoping that perhaps the drop and run was nothing more than a bedraggled babysitter in a rush and not something more.

Chad shook his head. "There's only Anya, at least so far as I know."

Ever so carefully, she kneeled down and shuffled around the tattered gray blanket that rested over the sleeping baby, in search of some sort of note or anything that would give away the identity of the child. She found nothing.

The baby rustled slightly, putting its little red fists over its face as it yawned. The baby's breath smelled of milk and newness.

Though Shaye didn't have much experience with babies, she guessed this little one was no more than a month or two old—far too young to be left out in the cold on some stranger's doorstep.

"How long have you guys lived here?" she asked, looking up and over her shoulder at Chad.

"Just a few months." He stared down at the baby, like he was trying to figure out exactly what it was.

Not long enough for this baby to have been his.

Though, if the baby was his, it didn't make her feel any less attracted to him. In fact, a dude holding a baby could be one hell of a sight to see—even swoonworthy.

"Go look outside—did they drop off a bag with the baby or anything?" she said, pointing toward the door as she tried to keep her panic and excitement in check.

He stepped out the front door and returned with a small blue diaper bag. He handed it to her like it might carry some communicable disease. His scrunched expression made her laugh. "Babies and dirty diapers aren't contagious."

The look on his face disappeared and was quickly replaced by mock annoyance. "I believe I know how babies are made. And dirty diapers, for that matter."

She laughed. "At least there are a couple of things I don't have to worry about explaining to you."

She could feel the warmth rise in her cheeks even though she was a damn adult. Why couldn't she just be a bit cooler under pressure...or in this case, when flirting?

Opening the bag, she pulled out a handful of store-brand diapers, generic formula, a little boy's onesie and a dirty burp cloth. There was nothing in the side pockets, or anywhere else, to indicate the baby's name, or where he had come from.

"What do you think we should do?" she asked, looking up at Chad with a diaper in her hand.

"First, don't look at me like that when you have a diaper in your hands," he teased.

She smirked as she dropped it back in the diaper bag. "Okay, does that make you feel better?"

He nodded, but his face had tightened, almost as if his teasing had simply been a mechanism he'd employed to give himself a moment to process her question. "I… We can't call anyone. At least not yet. First, we need to get out of here." He bit at the side of his cheek. "And I hate to say this, but it may be best if we simply drop him off at the hospital. They can contact the police and figure out where the kiddo came from."

"We're not dropping this kid off like he's some kind of orphan." She ran her fingers gently over the edge of the baby's car seat. He rustled in his sleep, letting out a sweet baby sigh. Though this baby was not really her problem, it didn't feel right to just abandon him for what would be the second time today.

Chad sighed. "I know he's cute. But what will we do with him? We're one step away from being on the run. In fact, we're literally in the middle of running away from hitmen.

Now isn't the time to bring a baby into any of it. Not only for his safety, but for our own."

Everything Chad said made absolute sense. But that didn't change the feeling that there was a reason he had been brought to their doorstep, a reason that neither of them understood.

"Chad, you're right." She searched for an excuse for them not to give up the child, at least not yet. "But all hospitals have cameras, even hospitals in little tiny towns like this. If we drop him off, we'll be on the radar."

"We are already on the radar, Shaye." He crossed his arms over his chest and leaned against the couch. He didn't need to finish his statement for her to know what he was thinking—that their being in danger was all her fault. She didn't need to be reminded.

"Chad, I know that you may think that I'm being crazy, but I think that for right now we should keep him." She gave Chad a pleading look, and as she did, she could see some of his resolve melt away.

Hopefully she wasn't making another mistake by begging for this child's reprieve.

There was just something about the baby's cherubic, chubby cheeks and plump little wrists that drew her. Perhaps it was her motherly instincts, but she had to protect this little one—at least until they found his mother, or learned why he had been left on their doorstep.

Chapter Eight

Chad locked the door of the ranch behind them and checked the cameras as he pulled the car seat higher up on his arm until the bar sat nestled in the crook of his elbow. Snow was sputtering down from the heavens, and as they walked toward the truck, he could see his breath. Gently, he pulled the blanket up higher around the baby, making sure that none of his delicate skin was exposed to the chill.

He still stood by what he'd said—the baby had no place in their life right now. But somehow, and he wasn't exactly sure how it had happened, they were now the proud caretakers of a mystery baby. He had one crazy life.

He strapped the car seat into the back seat of the pickup, which was way harder than dismantling and putting back together a rifle. As he sat back and inspected his work, he wasn't quite sure if he had put the belt in the right spot, and there were some random hooks that he had absolutely no idea about, but he was satisfied. He gave the car seat one more wiggle to make sure it was tight, and as he did, the baby jostled awake. His blue eyes were the color of the shallow Caribbean Sea. He had never seen a blue so pure and bright.

As the baby stared at him, a wide toothless grin appeared on his face. The little boy cooed and gurgled and then stuffed his tiny fist into his mouth, covering it with saliva.

Shaye stood beside him and smiled as the baby smacked and cooed. She had a soft, motherly look on her face as she peered at the baby, and he couldn't deny that she had never looked more beautiful to him.

He had not been the kind of man who dreamed of having a family, but standing here with Shaye at his side and a baby in the back seat, he couldn't deny that something about it just felt *right*. It was like Shaye was correct in assuming that whatever force, or culmination of events, that had put this baby in their lives had been right in doing so. It felt good to have this little carefree munchkin as part of their journey.

Unfortunately, it wouldn't last. But that didn't mean he couldn't enjoy the moment.

He took a long look at the baby and then

walked around to the passenger side of the truck and opened the door for Shaye. She gave the little one a tiny wave and blew him a kiss before making her way into the pickup and letting Chad close the door behind her.

As soon as he got in and started the pickup, Shaye turned to him. "Do you ever think about having a family?"

His entire body seized up. Though not a moment earlier he had imagined *them* as a family, he wasn't sure whether or not he dared to admit such a thought to her. Sure, there had definitely been some flirting, and, well…that kiss… But he wasn't quite ready to have the conversation about children. If they did, it was almost like they were taking their relationship to another level. And, truth be told, he was a bit relieved that the thing in the kitchen hadn't gone too much further.

If she had touched him one more time, he couldn't have resisted lifting her to the counter and showing her exactly how much he wanted her. He could almost imagine it now—her hair falling down over her shoulders as she leaned back and pressed herself against him. Her hands on the button of his pants, roaming downward until… And he could only dream of how good it would feel to experience all of her.

His body stirred to life.

Nope. He couldn't have those kinds of thoughts.

They were on the run. Not only that, but they were also now on the run with a baby. Everything in his life was a bad idea, and yet it seemed to be careening toward even more bad ideas around every curve. That said, just because something was a bad idea, it didn't mean he couldn't enjoy the hell out of it.

"Chad?" she asked, pulling his attention back to the snow-covered road in front of them and the question she had raised.

"Kids?" he said, his voice half-choked. "I like them."

Good. Vague. Noncommittal. He gave himself an imaginary pat on the back.

"I figured that much, Chad," Shaye said with a wave of her hand. "But what about having ones of your own?"

He gulped.

"What about you and Raj? Were you guys thinking about having kids?"

Avoidance. The second-best tool in his arsenal when dodging a question.

He was so nailing this.

And then he glanced over at Shaye. The glowing happiness that had taken over her features since the baby arrived seemed to seep out of her, replaced by a simmering unease.

Damn it. He shouldn't have brought up Raj. No doubt she had taken the mention of his name as a blow.

As he opened his mouth to offer an apology, she started to speak.

"Actually, Raj and I had talked about it. But we were together such a short time."

He collected himself. Okay, she wanted to talk about Raj and he hadn't hurt her feelings by mentioning his name. But now he wasn't entirely sure he had done the right thing in opening up this can of worms. After their kiss in the kitchen, talking about Raj made him deeply uncomfortable.

He would have never even met Shaye if it hadn't been for Raj and his love of her. If his friend was looking out at them from whatever beyond, would Raj even approve?

He shook off his thoughts. "You don't have to be married to start having kids. Or even if you wanted to wait, you have options." He stopped. It felt so weird talking about her getting knocked up by another man.

He inwardly groaned.

They *definitely* couldn't take things to a more intimate level again. Nope. No way. Not now. Not ever.

She gave a slight grimace, making him wonder if she felt just as uncomfortable with all this. "I understand that we *could* have decided to start having children, it's just that it never felt quite right. You know?"

No. He didn't really understand. The closest he had ever come to getting married was when he was… He tried to think of a time he had been tempted to ask a woman for her hand, but none of his former girlfriends had ever made the cut. Not that they weren't all amazing women—they were great. It was just that he had never met a woman who had fit into his crazy, erratic life.

That was, until he had met Shaye.

No. He reminded himself.

But if Shaye and Raj hadn't really felt the push to have kids, then why was she talking to him about having kids now?

"So what about you?" she persisted.

He rubbed the back of his neck, checking in the rearview mirror and catching a glimpse of the car seat. "I… Well, it's never been on the docket for me."

"How is that?"

"You know…never met the right woman. Never had a life that would lead to family living." He could feel his pulse quickening, thanks to her interrogation.

"Raj once told me that you were somewhat of a serial dater. How could you date all the time and never talk to one of your girlfriends about having kids?" she asked, giving him a pinched look, as if he had to be lying to her.

He didn't want to tell her that he normally didn't date the kind of women that were interested in having anything serious. He tended to be drawn to women who, just like him, didn't have a long-term commitment in mind—women who had just gotten out of serious relationships and were just looking for a rebound, or women who were young and unencumbered.

His last girlfriend had been thirty-two and recently divorced. They'd seen each other off and on for a few months while he had been bouncing between countries, but as soon as he left her apartment, she never really seemed to ask him where he was going. He would text her when he was back in town—they would go to dinner and occasionally things moved to the bedroom. But beyond laughing and telling stories about their day, their relationship really hadn't taken steps toward anything more. In fact, the only reason he had known her last name was because he did a background check before giving her his phone number.

They never really broke up, but then they had never really dictated the limitations or boundaries of the relationship. That was the way he had liked it. Until recently, he hadn't really considered he was the kind of guy who would be interested in anything more than a companion. And yet when he spent time with Shaye, he wanted something more than a dinner date. He wanted someone who was beyond a companion. He wanted someone who was a partner, but also a person who made him want to be a better man.

But he couldn't tell her any of that. Trying to explain how his former relationships worked seemed more dangerous than climbing Mount Kilimanjaro. The last thing he wanted was for Shaye to think any less of him, especially after what happened with Kash back at the party. But if he didn't open up to her, and tell her who he really was—imperfections and all—then he was making a conscious choice to wall her out. And if he wasn't going to open up to her, there was no chance there would ever be anything more between them. And he wouldn't be happy keeping her as a shirttail friend.

Come hell or high water, she needed to know him for who he really was.

"To be honest, Shaye, I don't recall ever

talking to a woman about having children. I don't typically find myself in relationships that were anything like what you and Raj had—you really loved each other."

She started picking at her fingernail as she looked down into her lap. "Things weren't perfect between us, but we did love each other. I miss him a lot."

He nodded. "I miss him, too. He was a good friend and a good man. You would have to search high and low to find a man worthy of you—a man as good as Raj will be hard to find."

He could feel her glance at him, but he kept his eyes firmly planted on the snow-covered road in front of them as he edged out onto the frontage road.

There was a long awkward silence between them. And he wished he could have taken back all of his talk of Raj and they could somehow have a conversation without so many land mines.

He glanced in his rearview mirror as a silver Suburban came racing down the road behind them and nearly attached itself to his rear bumper. He gritted his teeth as he tried to focus on the road and not the guy behind him.

"I didn't mean to upset you," Shaye said, having likely misinterpreted his anger.

"No, it's not that," he said, jabbing his thumb toward the car behind them. "The jerk behind us is in a big hurry, and doesn't seem to want to pass."

She turned around and looked out the back window toward the offending driver. "Just slow down—they'll eventually take a hint."

He eased off the gas, hoping that she was right. But instead of going around him, the dude driving crept closer to the back of their truck. How he was not actually scraping his bumper was a mystery.

Up ahead, on the left, was the road that led to the address that Zoey had stuffed in his hand. Once again, Chad checked the rearview, hoping somehow the guy had backed off, but the man was still right behind them. He was wearing dark sunglasses and a baseball cap pulled tight, hiding his face.

He didn't like the looks of the man. Instead of turning left, Chad didn't even slow down and stepped on the gas, causing the truck to fishtail slightly as he put space between them and the Suburban.

"What are you doing?" Shaye asked, clinching her hands in her lap nervously.

"This place is a small town," Chad said. "There are crappy drivers anywhere you go, but this is the kind of town where everybody knows everybody. You know, the it's kind of the place where if high-school Johnny is pulled over by the cops, his mom and dad are both gonna get phone calls long before the cop even leaves the driver-side window. And forget what will happen when he gets home." He forced a smile.

She gave a nervous laugh.

"I don't know who the guy is behind me, but if he was from around here, he wouldn't be driving like a complete ass." He readjusted the rearview mirror, hoping to get a glimpse of the guy's license plate, but it was covered with snow.

"I didn't know you had turned all country boy," Shaye said with a tight grin.

"Well, ma'am, I've always been country," he said, doing his best John Wayne impression. "A horse is a horse, it ain't gonna make a difference what color it is," he said.

"No. You, sir, are turning more country by the minute. You're not careful, the next thing I know is that you will be driving cattle and singing 'Git Along, Little Dogies.'"

"Ah, shucks, them's some high hopes for this little ol' cowpoke," he teased as he glanced back in the mirror. The Suburban was speeding up again. Chad sped up until he was doing seventy-five in a forty-five, but he wasn't putting much additional space between them and their tail. "Crap."

There was somebody in the back of the Suburban, and as he watched they climbed into the passenger seat. He wasn't completely sure, but he could have sworn he saw the glint of a rifle barrel as the man had moved.

They couldn't get into a shoot-out, not with Shaye and the baby in the truck. He hit the gas. The speedometer shot toward ninety miles an hour—far too fast for the road conditions.

"Chad, don't drive so fast," Shaye said, her voice tight.

"You need to grab the baby and get on the floor." The road blurred by as they screamed down the straight road that led to more and more ranch land and little else.

"Are you kidding me?" She gave him a disbelieving look. "There's no way I'm going to take that baby out of his car seat. What happens if we get in an accident? I couldn't live with myself if something happened to this little one."

"Those guys behind us have a gun. If they take a shot, the metal back there isn't thick enough to stop a bullet from penetrating and…" He didn't dare finish his sentence.

She unbuckled, turned around and reached

back, quickly unfastening the baby from the car seat. "Be careful, Chad. Please."

He was known for his driving skills, having gotten his various STEALTH members out of some extremely hairy situations, but that didn't mean accidents didn't happen—especially when the conditions were treacherous and icy.

She lifted the baby over the back of the seat and crouched down on the floorboard in front of the passenger seat, encircling the child with her body. She looked up and her eyes were filled with terror.

"It'll be okay, Shaye," he said, hoping to make her feel better. "I'm just being extra cautious."

She nodded, but remained silent.

He had no idea who these bastards were, but he had to get Shaye and the baby to safety and as far away as humanly possible. The road stretched out in front of them like a white snake, making slow bends right and left toward the mountains in the distance. To their right, ahead was the highway. It ran parallel to the frontage road just for a few miles and then the two roads forked apart. Between this brief pairing of snakes was a thin, barbed-wire fence.

He was tempted, but did he dare go

through it, hit the highway and get the hell out of there? If they managed to make it onto the highway without popping a tire, getting stuck, or spinning out on the ice and snow between the roads, maybe the plan would work. But just *maybe*. He wasn't sure it was worth the risk.

If something happened, they would be sitting ducks. All the bastards would have to do is get close and pull the trigger, and everything would be lost.

He silently reminded himself that he had been through worse and made it to the other side. This was far better than the firefight he had been caught up in Aleppo. He and Raj had been taking rounds from all sides while escaping after a contract hit. They had thought their team had neutralized their opposition, but as soon as they hit the streets, hellfire had started raining down on them, as tracer rounds had zipped by, inches from their heads.

But then he hadn't had a baby and a woman he cared for in tow. He and Raj had known what they were getting themselves into. And though Shaye may have had a clue about how dangerous his world could be, he was sure she hadn't come here thinking she'd be attacked around every corner. Between this and the hardware store, it almost seemed like the entire world had it out for them.

He had promised Raj that if anything happened to him he would keep the woman Raj loved safe.

That was one promise that, now more than ever, he couldn't break.

Chapter Nine

Over the years, Shaye had been tied up, held hostage and had her life threatened, but she had never been more frightened than she was in this moment. She hugged the baby tighter against her chest, cooing in his ear in hopes of keeping him calm.

His eyes were wide open and he shifted restlessly, pushing against her hold like she was the one who wished him harm. The baby let out an ear-piercing wail. "Shh, little one, it's going to be okay." Shaye rocked the child as much as the tight space would allow. "I'm here. I've got you." But as she said the words, she couldn't help the sense of impotence that overtook her.

As it was, she couldn't even keep herself safe. Everything about their situation screamed of their inability to adequately take care of this baby. Though she had wanted to keep him, at least until things were straightened out, she couldn't deny that they had made the wrong choice. If only she had called the police and had them come and pick up the baby.

Why did the choices always seem so much clearer in retrospect? Not for the first time, she wished life came with a manual.

The truck lurched violently with the crunch of metal on metal as they were struck from behind.

"Son of a…" Chad said, reaching out his arm toward them as if to press them down into the footwell.

Though she was more than aware that his arm wouldn't stop any real injury, his closeness made her feel safer.

"Are you okay?" Chad asked, his words fast.

She nodded and looked down at the baby, who was still squealing in her arms. The little one's wails turned into a drone of crying. "Screw this," she said, getting up off the floor and into the passenger seat. She tucked the baby's blanket tightly around him, protecting him from the cold air, and then opened up the passenger-side window.

"What are you doing?" Chad asked.

"Hand me your gun. I'm not going to sit

down there and do nothing. We're in this together. Together, we are going to fight."

He unclipped the gun on his ankle and handed it over.

She leaned out the window, tucking the baby under one arm and bracing herself against the back of the seat. She pointed in the general direction of the Suburban.

The man in the passenger seat started to move, as if he was raising his gun, but before he could do anything, she fired. The gunshot ripped through the air, the sound booming around her like an invisible mushroom cloud.

The Suburban swerved, but it was too late. Steam poured out of the radiator.

Pride welled within her. Though she had never shot a gun before, she had hit her target.

And yet, they didn't stop.

"I think I got him," she cried.

Chad stared up at the mirror. "It looks like you struck the radiator. It won't be long before their car overheats. But they can still go a couple miles before they'll be forced to stop."

She moved to lean out the window and take another shot, but Chad stopped her.

"No," he said. "I don't want you getting

hurt. Whoever these guys are, they aren't in-experienced. I don't want you getting shot."

She sank down in her seat and rolled up the truck's window. She pulled the baby against her chest and gently ran her fingers over his head as she shushed him. As she looked up from the helpless child in her arms, the Suburban rammed them. The force of the hit sent them into a full fishtail. The world blurred around her, and as Chad tried to regain control, the truck skidded off the road and screeched against the barbed-wire fence, which collapsed under them. The front tires hit the side of the highway and the rumble strip before Chad had a chance to recover and he jerked, overcorrecting. Even with the snow on the ground, their tires squealed on the highway as they spun in a half circle.

The baby went silent and she wasn't sure if she should be relieved or concerned. She glanced down, and he had gone rigid in her arms, his eyes wide open and his little mouth a perfect *O*.

"My feelings exactly, little guy," she said, as Chad regained control of the truck.

They hurtled back toward Mystery, having done a complete 180. Thankfully, the high-way appeared to be empty of traffic.

Behind them, working through the snow

and downed fence, was the Suburban. It was pouring steam from the front of its grille, but as the driver merged onto the highway, the vehicle didn't appear to have lost any power.

Chad had the gas pedal pressed to the floor, but even with that, the Suburban was gaining on them. The man in the passenger seat leaned out the window. In his arms was a large, long gun. She didn't know much about weapons, but it looked like a rifle that the military would use—one with automatic shooting capabilities.

She wasn't wrong.

Chad reached over and pressed her downward, so she was completely covering the baby just as a smattering of gunfire rang out. She heard the ping as bullets struck the tailgate and then the shattering of glass as a round pierced the back window.

The shooting stopped.

She looked up at the windshield. It had been hit from behind several times, one just mere inches away from Chad's head.

Her breath caught in her throat.

"Chad," she said, breathlessly staring at the bullet hole.

"I know," Chad said, "but I'm okay. Every-thing's gonna be okay. It looks like they're slowing down." He jabbed his thumb in the direction behind them.

"Do you want me to call the police?" she yelled over the whistle of the wind through their open-air truck.

Chad chewed on the inside of his cheek. He glanced up at the mirror, like he was assessing just exactly how much trouble they were in. "No, we just need to give them a few miles for their vehicle to overheat and stay out of their line of fire. Then we can call Wyatt."

"But don't you think that by now Wyatt has his hands full with the incident at the hardware store?"

Chad sighed. "It would look awful strange if first they have a murder, and now they have a high-speed car chase and shoot-out. I'd rather we not be tied to any of it."

She nodded, but thought about their earlier mistake in not calling the police about the baby. "I think you're right about this guy," she said, nodding toward the child. "It would've been better if we had turned him over to someone else."

She looked in the side mirror at the Suburban as they roared down the highway. The cloud of steam pouring out of the engine had grown, obscuring the driver from her view.

Finally, she and Chad seemed to be putting a bit of distance between them.

"See that road sign there?" Chad asked, pointing toward a turnoff they had passed on the frontage road.

The sign read Mockingbird Heights.

"What about it?" she asked, staring out at the road as they passed it by.

"That's the road where the other bug-out cabin is. I think it's tucked back in there a couple of miles."

A sense of excitement crept up inside her belly. "Do you think your family saw the chase? Maybe your brothers are on the way to help?"

Chad shook his head. "I don't know. Why don't you give Zoey a call and let her know that we have some bogies."

"Bogies? As in *Top Gun* bogies?" She let out a nervous, scared laugh.

"Are you really going to make fun of my eighties reference at a time like this?" he teased, giving her a half grin as he checked the mirror.

Their assailants were falling farther and farther behind and now the steam was completely enveloping the car.

He passed her his unlocked cell phone, Zoey's name highlighting the screen like he had already pressed the call button.

Was he handing her the phone to avoid talking to his sister?

"Oh, no… You're not going to make me the fall guy on this one," she said, pressing the speaker button as the phone rang.

"What? No. I—" Chad said.

"Where the hell are you guys? Are you Flintstoning your way over here or what?"

Apparently dated pop-culture references ran in the family. It only made her like them more.

She gave Chad a look to tell him that he needed to deal with this.

"Uh, I'll take the or-what option," Chad said, chuckling nervously.

"What in the hell is that supposed to mean?" Zoey grumbled.

"It means that we met up with a couple of guys in a Suburban who seemed hell-bent on filling us up with holes." Chad shifted in the driver's seat like it was getting hot underneath him. "The last thing I want to do right now is lead them, or anyone else who may be with them, straight to our bug-out location."

There was a long moment of silence on the other end of the line. "Did you neutralize the threat?" Zoey finally asked.

"Kinda," he said, wiggling again.

The baby let out a wail.

"What? And what was that sound?" Zoey asked.

She and Chad looked at each other and a stone dropped in her belly. She had forgotten that Zoey didn't know about the baby just yet.

"Well, um…" Chad began, as Shaye leaned back and rifled around in the diaper bag until she found a pacifier and plopped it into the baby's mouth.

He took the blue plastic nub and sucked at it greedily, making Shaye wonder if the baby wasn't so much frightened as he was hungry, or maybe just reacting to the terror around him.

"Someone dropped a baby off on the doorstep of the ranch," Shaye said, helping out Chad.

"You have to be kidding me." Zoey was the one who now sounded breathless. "And you have this baby with you, why?"

"Seriously? You wouldn't expect us to leave a baby on the doorstep of a house that was about to be under siege, would you?" Chad asked, his voice tight and rigid with anger.

"Of course not," Zoey said, and Chad appeared to relax ever so slightly in his seat.

"But you don't think bringing a baby over here is a good idea, do you? And what about the dudes shooting at you? What about the baby?"

Finally, it sounded as if Zoey was putting all the pieces together.

"Jeez," Zoey said, letting out a long exhale. "Where are you guys now?"

"We are by mile marker seventeen, heading north toward Mystery," Chad said.

"And the guys who were following you?" Zoey asked.

"Well…that's the other part." Chad ran his hand over his face. "They broke down. Shaye shot out their radiator and they overheated. I was hoping you could catch up to them and finish what we started."

Shaye hated to think about what exactly Chad meant by that, but at the same time, the men had shot at them and a child—whatever they got, they deserved.

"And where are they now?" Zoey asked.

"Unfortunately, they are near mile marker nineteen." Chad cleared his throat.

"But that's… Are you kidding me right now?" Zoey spat. "Were you trying to lead them straight to us? What the hell, Chad?"

"It wasn't like we were trying to do anything other than get away. Just go take care of it, Zoey."

Shaye turned around and took one last look at the Suburban that was growing smaller and smaller as they drove away. She'd been so proud of her shot, and now once again, she'd screwed things up. When was she ever going to do anything right?

No, she wasn't going to feel bad about this. They had saved the baby from any harm, gotten away from their enemies and delivered the men almost straight into STEALTH's hands. In her book that could be counted as a win.

Chapter Ten

When they made it back to Mystery, the town was abuzz with people coming and going as they left work and went about their shopping. But outside the hardware store, on Main Street, was a coroner's van and two police cars. Chad cringed.

Though he was nearly positive no one had seen them at the hardware store, he couldn't say the same about what had just happened on the highway. The odds were stacked against them that with all of the nonsense that had happened today, they had gone unnoticed.

Hopefully the cleanup crew had done their job and wiped the place clean of anything that could have put him and Shaye at the scene. If not, well…he couldn't think about that.

"I think the baby needs a change," she said, rubbing at her nose like she was trying to waft away some foul odor.

As he spoke, the stale air invaded his senses.

"Whew," he said with a nod, "you are right about that one. It shouldn't take us too long to get to the new place, but do you think he can wait that long?"

There was a ripple of small explosions inside the boy's diaper.

Shaye laughed. "If that sound is any indication, I think he's not quite done yet. A few minutes or so won't make a huge difference. But I don't want him going too long." She nuzzled the baby's cheek with her nose. "We don't want you getting diaper rash, now do we?"

Checking to make sure that no one else was following them and their six was clear, he turned toward the road leading to their new hideout. He glanced back at the end of pickup bed. Even from where he sat, he could make out a series of dents where the Suburban had crashed into them. Hopefully no one in town had noticed the damage—or the bullet holes that riddled the cab.

The more he thought about how many loose ends were out there, the deeper the pit in his stomach became. There was no way, with everything stacked against them, that they weren't going to attract attention .

If only he knew who the men in the Suburban were.

He was tired of sitting idly by, waiting for the attack. He wanted to go on the offensive.

He had been in on the meeting when they had all decided to face whatever came their way, but now, with so many people depending on him to provide protection and safety, he wasn't sure that they had done the right thing. He couldn't help feeling like they were sitting ducks. Now that the world was crashing down on them, their idea to stay and face their enemies seemed naive.

But he wasn't sure he could convince Zoey to change their strategy.

"What are you thinking about?" Shaye asked.

Whenever one of his former girlfriends had asked him that question, he had always hated it. But hearing the question from Shaye, he didn't feel the same way.

"I was thinking about dumping this truck. The guys back there, they can identify it now—especially with it being all shot up." He reached over and put his arm behind her, pulling her and the baby closer. "And, more importantly, I was thinking about how we're going to keep everybody safe."

She tucked into him. She didn't say anything, which surprised him. And yet he appreciated that she wasn't offering any sort of platitude, or trying to convince him that everything would be all right. As of right now, their future was up in the air. It would only be a matter of time until the men and women gunning for them would be upon their doorstep.

"You know," Shaye said, sitting up with a start as she reached down into her purse and pulled out a set of car keys, "my rental is parked just up the street. We could take it. Maybe dump the truck?"

He reached over and gave her a peck on the head as a sense of relief welled in him. "You are a real lifesaver, you know that?"

"I don't know if I agree with that," she said. "I'm part of the reason you're in this mess."

He shook his head. "Don't talk like that. One way or another, hellfire was going to come raining down on us. Maybe it was a day sooner than we expected, but it was coming. I don't want you to feel bad. For all we know, your being here may have saved us in the long run. I've always believed that there's a reason for everything."

Shaye looked out the window, and he wondered if he had said the wrong thing—though it had been a while since she had lost Raj, she would likely never be entirely over his death.

"I usually hate when people say that," she said. "At Raj's funeral, people kept telling me that there was some sort of plan, a reason for his death. Every time someone spoke those words, I wanted to scream." She sucked in a breath and held it for a long moment before slowly exhaling. "But here, now, with you… I'm wondering if they were right."

He held her tight, nuzzling his nose in her hair, taking in the sweet perfume of her honest vulnerability.

"Whatever happens, we're in this thing together." He smoothed her hair behind her ear as he pulled the truck down the alley behind the buildings on Main Street and parked.

He grabbed the gun and all their personal items, then threw them in the diaper bag before flinging the bag over his shoulder and helping Shaye and the baby down from the cab of the truck. "Be careful, there's a big step," he said, holding her hand.

Shaye smiled at him, and some of the sadness that was always in her eyes seemed to lighten. If nothing else, their time together could finally complete her healing. He may not have been her hero, but at least he could provide her with something.

They made their way over to the rental car, carefully steering clear of the hardware store and the crowd that had gathered to watch the coroner and police as they removed the innocent man's body. He wasn't sure whose squad car sat outside the building, but he hoped it was Wyatt's. More importantly, he hoped that they had deemed the man's death nothing more than an accident—and that Zoey and their team had set it up so that the man's family would be taken care of. If he had his way, his family would be receiving a large, unexpected life insurance check from a strange company.

It was a quiet ride to their new place. As they were about to turn down the snow-covered lane, he spotted the deserted Suburban sitting on the side of the highway. The men from inside were nowhere to be seen. Hopefully Zoey and his brothers had gotten to them before they got away. If they had, and if they had left them alive, maybe they could get some much-needed information.

As they slowed down to turn, she looked up at him. "Do you think…?"

She didn't have to finish her sentence for him to know what she was asking.

He shrugged.

She didn't complete her thought. And as they drove deeper into the enclave of mountains, a towering log cabin came into view.

Around the outside of the house was a wrap-around deck complete with a railing comprised of plasma cut steel panels shaped into moose, bear and elk. The black steel stood in deep contrast to the white snow that drifted around the deck as the wind blew down off the mountains.

Chad had no idea to whom the home belonged, but whoever built it must have been affluent, and around here, it wouldn't have surprised him if it was some ski house for a Hollywood star.

He glanced over at Shaye and caught her smiling as she looked toward the house and gave an approving nod. Though the house was beautiful, he didn't really care about its aesthetic qualities. More importantly, everyone he loved was inside and protected.

As they ascended the driveway leading to the house, he was relieved to find that the house itself was perched on a knoll, giving those inside a better vantage than those on the ground. No doubt, Zoey had taken it into consideration when she had chosen this spot. Though he and Zoey didn't always see eye-to-eye, she was incredibly intelligent. Maybe he had been wrong in questioning her plan, after all.

As they grabbed their gear and walked up

the steps leading to the front door, it opened. Jarrod looked down on them as they approached. "Glad to see you both could finally join us."

"You can't be half as relieved as we are." Chad gave his brother a smack on the arm as he waited for him to move out of the way.

Jarrod took the diaper bag from Chad and dropped it inside the door. "Is that the baby everyone is talking about?" Jarrod asked, opening up his arms and motioning to take a child. "You know his name?"

Shaye's smile reappeared. "No idea. We really haven't been calling him anything."

"If this little guy's gonna hang out here, he's gotta have a name," Jarrod said, taking the baby. He made a pinched face as the smell reached his nose. "Little one, you are one stinky dude." He laughed, running his finger down the baby's cheek. "I think for now, we should call you Pig-Pen."

She shook her head. "That's a terrible name."

"Nothing from *Peanuts* is terrible," Jarrod teased. "By the way, Shaye, it's nice to officially meet you. I'm glad you're here."

Shaye looked slightly taken aback at Jarrod's warm reception, but Chad was grateful for his brother's gesture.

"Thanks, Jarrod," Shaye said with a nod. "Though, I must say, I'm sorry for all the upheaval I've caused."

"Upheaval is the name of the game in this family." Jarrod waved her off. He looked down at the baby as he rocked him gently. "And as for this little guy, I think we should call him Peanut for now. We can't have a nameless baby on our hands."

"Regardless of his name, we shouldn't have a baby on our hands. Period," Zoey said, walking down the hall that led to the great room. Her voice echoed out from the corridor like she was speaking down upon them, commanding them from high. "We need to protect the innocent. Anya is staying at Dunrovin with our cousins—I fear there may be more danger coming our way."

"Did you catch the men who were chasing us?" Chad asked.

Zoey nodded, giving Jarrod a knowing look. "The men are currently here. Trevor is with them."

"Here," Jarrod said, reaching for the diaper bag. "I'll take Peanut and get him changed. I'm sure that Mindy will want to see this little one. She has a major case of baby fever going on right now." He cooed at the baby as he walked off in the direction that Zoey had come from.

Just talking about sending the baby away filled him with a strange loneliness. It was kind of nice having a little one around. Babies took a huge amount of work and attention, and in this case added more fear to an already fraught situation, but there was no question about the love he had started to feel for the little one.

It would likely nearly kill him when they returned him.

But he couldn't deny that his life was no place for a child.

As if validating his thoughts, a man's yell rippled out from deep in the house, the sound filled with rage and hate. Shaye moved closer to him, and he could feel her body tense beside him.

"Have you found out who sent them?"

Zoey nodded. "They're not talking but they both have the Gray Wolves brand on their arms, so I have little doubt that they were sent here by Bayural. And, from what I've been able to pull from the cell phones, they were in direct contact with someone from Turkey while they were in pursuit of you." She paused, looking down at the floor for a moment like she was trying to summon the strength to say what Chad was already thinking. "It is only a matter of time now."

He reached down and took Shaye's hand, giving his sister an acknowledging nod. There were no words for the sense of foreboding that filled him. And all he could think about was whether this acceptance was what Trish had felt in the moments before her death, when the sickle rested upon her soul and darkness loomed.

They could fight against the Gray Wolves, but even with their resources, there was little chance they could win. Bayural's men and women didn't wear uniforms. They didn't fight by rules. They didn't have a certain look. They weren't driven by morals or obligations—only money. And money was the one thing that Bayural seemed to have an endless supply of.

"But there is some good news," Zoey said. "I've called in our operatives and taken on a few new employees. Our teams should be arriving throughout the next couple of days. So far, I've assigned about twenty guards to the perimeter of the house. As of now, the family is on lockdown. No one is to come or go from this compound."

Shaye grabbed his hand harder, leaned in and whispered, "It suddenly feels as if I'm back with my father at the palace. I can't say that I like it."

He couldn't deny that suddenly it felt as though they were a country under fire.

He turned to her. "Shaye, I think you should consider either finding another place to go, or at least going to Dunrovin with Anya and Sarge, until this is all over. I don't want to put you in any more danger than you are already in."

She let go of his hand. She looked to Zoey and then back at him like she wanted to say something but was afraid of speaking freely in front of his sister.

Zoey cleared her throat. "Excuse me, I need to go and check on things with Trevor. In the meantime, Chad—I'm serious. I don't want you going anywhere."

The expression *sitting duck* came to mind. He had only just arrived at this place, and yet he already felt as if he was going stir-crazy. He'd never been one to accept boundaries well. But he understood why Zoey was acting the way she was. They couldn't keep running. Come hell or high water, being constantly on the run had to come to an end. They couldn't keep letting Bayural and his teams of mercenaries dictate what they were or weren't going to do with their lives. Bayural had already taken Trish—he couldn't have the rest of them.

As Zoey retreated, he suddenly couldn't stop looking at his hands. "It's not that I don't want you here. I hope you know that," he said. The sharp expression on Shaye's face stopped him.

"But it's convenient to push me away, I get it." She slipped her hands into his. "I told you, Chad, I'm not going anywhere. We are a team and we are in this together. Whatever happens to you, happens to me. Like it or not, I'm a part of this now. From the sound of things, you are going to need as many hands as possible to fight this battle."

"I made a promise to Raj. I told him that I would always protect you." He reached up and pushed a stray hair out of her face and away from her beautiful chocolate-colored eyes. "I already lost my sister to this enemy. I know what he and his people are capable of. They won't think anything about killing you. And I think even your father knows it— that's why he sent his men to retrieve you."

"So you agree with my father?" There was an edge of antagonism in her voice.

Crap. There was no way he could get out of this situation without making her even angrier.

"I guess, if it means keeping you safe."

She swiveled on her heel. As she moved to walk away, she looked back at him. "It's been a long day. If you need me, I'm going to find myself a bed and take a nap before I say something that I'll regret. I recommend you do the same."

Chapter Eleven

It was a long night, and early the next morning, Shaye heard footsteps outside her bedroom door. She prayed for it to be Chad.

Just knock. Tell me you're sorry. That you want me.

But it remained silent. For a moment, she considered calling out and telling him to come in. But she couldn't make the first move. He had made it clear exactly how he felt—he cared about her, but he was Raj's friend, first and foremost. And as such, he would never be anything more to her.

And she couldn't begrudge him for it. On so many fronts, she understood. The betrayal of Raj's memory sat like a bitter pill on the tip of her tongue. But she couldn't help her growing feelings for Chad. If anything, having him around was like having a piece of Raj with her all the time. Though they were very different men, they had the same heroic spirit at their core. Each would have done nearly anything to keep her safe, and what they felt was right—even if doing the right thing was at odds with their own feelings.

At least, she assumed Chad was at odds with his own feelings.

She had hoped that their kiss was real. It had certainly felt oh, so real. There was an undeniable attraction between them, and yet maybe he considered it a mistake. Maybe he was simply swept up in the moment, and his other brain had taken over his thinking for a moment. Maybe once he came back to his senses, guilt had taken the place of desire.

And as much as she cared for him, she didn't want to be the reason he felt like he was betraying his friend, nor did she want to be a reason for him to feel guilty...or to agree with her father.

Maybe she should go away. She could build a different life. She could pretend she wasn't the daughter of a tyrant. She could pretend she hadn't lost all those she loved. She could pretend she hadn't fallen for a man who should have been strictly out of bounds.

But that was all it could be—nothing but pretend.

She opened her mouth to call out, but

stopped as the footsteps moved away from her door.

He must have been as confused by this as she was. Maybe it was better that they just stayed apart. Maybe she was the one who needed to clear her mind and start thinking with her head instead of her heart.

A sickening sadness filled her at the sound of his retreating.

She got out of bed and walked to the door. She pressed her hands against the cold wood and dropped her forehead to the paneling. It didn't make sense, but she missed him…and she wanted him here.

There was a knock from the other side of the panel, the vibration against her skin making her jump.

"Uh, yes?" she asked, moving back from the door.

Had Chad come back? Had he changed his mind? Did that mean that he wanted to make things right between them?

"You awake?" a woman said from the other side of the door.

Her stomach sank as the excitement seeped from her. "Uh, yeah, come in." She grabbed a sweater and threw it on over her pajamas as the door opened and Mindy walked in carrying the sleeping baby.

Shaye smiled at the sweet sight of the cherubic baby, his arms akimbo and a smile trembling at the corners of his dreaming lips.

How easy it was to love a child.

Maybe someday she would have one of her own, one who would look as peaceful and serene as he did.

"How is he doing?" she asked in a whisper as she moved to the bed and patted it for Mindy to sit down.

"Oh, he's the easiest baby. Once we got him changed and fed, he went right to sleep. He slept most of the night. I think he was a tired little Peanut."

"Oh, so the name stuck, did it?" Shaye asked, gently stroking the baby's head as Mindy gently rocked him.

Mindy inhaled the baby's scent, like she was soaking in all the baby she could. "For now, but I wonder what his real name is. He looks like he could be a Gavin or maybe a Lincoln. He's just so darn cute." She hugged him closer.

"He is such a beautiful boy," Shaye said.

"In truth, I wouldn't mind adding him to our family." Mindy looked up and gave her a conspiratorial grin. "You know, Jarrod and I are talking about starting a family. I think he's still on the fence, but this little guy may give him the push he needs." She looked down at the baby. "In fact, I think he wouldn't even mind if we adopted this one—if the stars aligned."

Shaye had been doing her best to try and not get overly attached to the baby, but she could see that she wasn't the only one struggling. "I hear you. It's hard not to want to take him in your arms and never let him go."

As she said it, it dawned on her that she could say the same thing about Chad—and the reality was, just like the baby, she was going to have to let Chad go.

"The men we love have a way of doing that to us, don't they?" Mindy asked, sending her a knowing smile.

"Is it that obvious?" Shaye asked, her cheeks warming with embarrassment.

"A woman like you doesn't travel halfway across the world just so she can hang out." Mindy smiled down at the baby like she was telling him a secret. "You can try and tell us that you just needed a safe place, but with your connections around the globe, we all know that there were at least a thousand other places that you could have landed…not that we aren't glad to have you here," she added.

"I don't think the entire family is happy with my being here, but thank you." She ran her hands over her fleece pajama bottoms. "You would be surprised how people drift away when you ostracize yourself from the prime minister of a country. I didn't have a lot of options."

"Was the man from the hardware store involved with your father?" Mindy asked.

She nodded. "I'm assuming that was obvious, as well?"

Mindy gave her a soft smile. "It wasn't a big leap. Your father is a tyrant, but he cares about you—which is admirable—even if he does go about showing it in entirely the wrong ways."

"Yes, killing my husband was the wrong way to show he cared." Her words came out sharper and more accurate than she had intended. But thoughts of her mother collided with Mindy's words. "That's just one of the reasons I can't be with Chad, now or ever. Clearly my father's still singularly focused on controlling my life." And maybe killing her. "I can't put Chad in danger."

"I don't think you can stop falling for Chad, or he can stop falling for you, no matter what the danger. It's obvious you have feelings for each other, so denying them you isolate yourself and only diminish your capabilities to stand up against your father. United you stand…" Mindy stood up with the baby and walked toward the window. "One thing I've learned about the Martins is that the source of their power isn't Zoey, or Chad, or Jarrod, or Trevor, or in any individual within their STEALTH team. Rather, their power lies in the fact that regardless of what life throws at them, they stand united. Trish's death could have torn them apart, and for a while it looked like it might, and yet they've struggled through, more powerful than ever."

"Do you really think that Chad is over her death?" Shaye asked.

"You would know more than I about how Chad is feeling. But I think he's had a harder time than the others because of his unique bond with Trish. Jarrod said that Chad and Trish were so close as babies that they even had a secret language. There's a bond between twins. And I'm sure, no matter how much time goes by, Chad will always have a void."

But was that void too big for him to love her?

"I hate to say it, but do you think two people can be too broken to love?"

Mindy shook her head. "I think love is like a bone. It can be broken, it can be cut, it can grow weak and brittle, but if you give it everything it needs it can recover and become stronger than it ever had been before."

She didn't want to be a cynic, but she couldn't help herself. "What about when we grow old and our bones weaken?"

"They may have changed, but just like love, they are the foundation of our being. Without them, we would be nothing."

Now there Mindy had a point.

They sat there in silence for a long moment as Shaye digested all that Mindy had told her. Her mind kept swirling back to love and relationships. Chad was scarred by his past, but so was she. It would be unwise and hypocritical for her to begrudge him when she herself had baggage. In fact, every person had baggage—hers was just in the form of her past and her family. Where Chad's family's love strengthened and built him up, her father's was like a cancer that threatened to bring her down.

But she would fight.

There was another knock on the door.

What was this place, a meeting room?

She laughed at herself as she walked over and opened the door.

Chad and Zoey were standing side by side, and Chad looked like the cat who had swallowed the canary. The look on his face made her wonder what kind of verbal condemnation Zoey had administered before they had arrived.

"What's wrong?" Shaye asked. His gaze refused to meet hers as she stared at him.

Zoey lifted her cell phone up like it was going on public display. "I pulled the video surveillance files from the Widow Maker Ranch's eyes-in-the-sky." Zoey clicked on a few buttons and sat down on the hope chest at the end of the bed. "After you told me about someone dropping off the baby, I thought I might be able to identify the person who had left him."

Had Zoey identified the baby's mother or guardian? Is that why Chad looked so upset? Did he have something to do with this baby? Something he wasn't telling her? She tried to stomp out the panic that rose within her.

No matter what, if the baby was Chad's, or if he knew the mother, or whatever…it was going to be okay. They could get through this. If he was the baby's father, they could even talk about incorporating the little one into their lives as they moved forward. That was *if* they ever truly had a relationship.

Or maybe he wouldn't want more encumbrances in his life. A baby and a new girlfriend… Maybe it would all be too much for him.

And what if he didn't know if he wanted to keep the baby? What if he put it up for adoption?

She glared at him, but as she did, she realized she was being ridiculous. She took a deep breath. She was getting ahead of herself.

Shaye paced around the room as Zoey tapped away on her phone.

It's going to be okay, she repeated to herself over and over with every quick step she took.

"Here, I got it." Zoey held up her phone for all to see.

There, standing beneath the lens of the camera, was a dark-haired woman with olive-hued skin and enormous black sunglasses covering most of her face. Her lips were the color of ripe blackberries and by all measures she was beautiful.

Was she one of Chad's exes?

If she was, it made Shaye wonder why he would ever be interested in a woman like herself. She wasn't ugly by any means, but in comparison to the virtual supermodel on Zoey's screen…well, she was at best a two out of ten.

No, she couldn't be so hard on herself.

Maybe she wasn't a two. When she dressed up and squeezed her butt into her Spanx, she was at least a solid four…maybe even a five. And a good pair of heels could turn her up maybe even another point on the hotness scale.

Chad stared at the women in the image, but he said nothing.

Zoey pressed the phone toward him. "Do you know who she is?" she asked, as if she also wondered if he was somehow connected to the woman and the baby.

Chad swallowed hard.

Shaye wasn't entirely sure, but her heart may have actually seized in her chest.

Was he afraid of making her feel bad by admitting he knew the woman—that he may have been the baby's father?

She had to sit down, so she stepped over to the hope chest and flopped down beside Zoey.

"Well?" Zoey persisted.

"I… I'm not sure," Chad started. "But I don't think I know her."

Shaye let out a long exhale.

"Have you seen her before?" Zoey asked.

Chad shook his head. "It's hard to tell with the sunglasses, but she doesn't look familiar."

Zoey glared at him. "If you don't know her,

then why in the hell would she leave a baby on your doorstep?"

Chad bristled. "First, it's not just *my* doorstep. It's *ours*. Did anyone even stop and think about that for a freaking moment?" His voice boomed as his anger exploded into rage.

Shaye instantly felt guilty. With the thing with Kash's sister, Kayla, and the fistfight, she had jumped to the conclusion that there were probably other skeletons in his closet, as well. Based on the facial expressions of his sister and his sister-in-law, they must have been following the same line of thinking.

Which didn't make her feel any better.

Here she had been consumed with whether or not she had feelings for this man, but at the same time she was making him out to be a person he wasn't.

She had been foolish.

And now he was the one paying the price, a victim of their assumptions. She wanted to pull him into her arms and tell him that she was sorry, that she had him all wrong. And yet, he would likely never grant her forgiveness for her stupidity.

After this, she could never be his…no matter how badly she wanted him.

Chapter Twelve

Had they all thought him capable of doing something like fathering a child and keeping it a secret? Or perhaps not knowing about the baby?

Sure, he had made his fair share of mistakes, but none was bigger than what had happened with Kayla. And in his defense, it wasn't like had been alone in the bed. She had been searching for a companion, a one-night stand as luck had it, just as badly as he had.

It had blossomed into something more for her, but to him it was only physical. The more they talked, the more Kayla had wanted more from him—and emotional attachment wasn't something he could provide then…maybe not even now.

He looked over at Shaye, who was giving him an apologetic look. He wanted to forgive her for assuming the worst of him, but the damage was already done. Like the rest of his family, she must have thought he was just a player. Didn't she know him better than that?

He was surprised by how much her incorrect judgment of him hurt.

Zoey tapped on her phone. "I'll look deeper into the woman's identity, but so far I've not been able to pull anything up. I'm thinking those sunglasses were no accident. But sunglasses or no, give me time and I'm sure I can get something."

"In the meantime," Chad began, "maybe you should go talk to Trevor and Jarrod. Maybe they have an idea who the woman may be."

Mindy looked slightly hurt at his suggestion and she started to make her way toward the door.

Before she could escape, he had to say something—something that didn't make him come off like he was totally insensitive, or worse, making assumptions about his brothers that were only too much like those about him.

"Not that the baby is one of theirs," he said, but it sounded weak coming from his lips. He stepped in Mindy's way and looked down at the baby.

Peanut looked like most babies, with round

little cheeks and ruddy, long fingers. He had never understood why, upon a new baby's birth, everyone always insisted that the baby "had their father's nose" or "their mother's eyes." To him, all babies looked cute, but one step up from a chimpanzee's offspring when they were born.

As he searched the baby's features for anything familiar, a giveaway of some sort that would definitely tie him to their lineage, he found nothing. He was a baby. A sweet, cuddly baby who beckoned to be held and played with, but a baby nonetheless.

Mindy looked up at him with a thin-lipped expression. "You know as well as I do that anything is possible—just look at the situation with Anya."

He swallowed back his guilt as he thought about how thoughtless he had been in condemning anyone for having a secret baby.

His niece had been introduced into their life as a child that no one had known existed. And for all Chad knew, perhaps he was the boy's biological father. Just because he didn't recognize the woman who had left the baby, didn't mean he didn't know the baby's mother. Maybe she was someone's sister, or even just the person who had been given the child to deliver to their feet.

Some of his animosity toward the women in the room slipped away. Though he had a right to be angry at them, it would be stupid to continue with his indignation—what would he say if their assumptions turned out to be correct?

He hadn't followed up on every one-night stand or chance encounter with women he'd been with—not that there had been that many. But anything was possible…and sometimes what seemed obvious was far from it.

He took a long, deep breath and slowly exhaled, like the simple motion could relieve him of the rest of his pent-up anxiety.

"Regardless of whose baby this is, he needs us. And for right now, I think we should focus on his safety and find him a safer place to live until we have everything sorted out with the Gray Wolves." He kneeled down and sniffed the boy's head as he gave him a soft peck. He smelled like the powdery scent of a fresh diaper.

Though he knew it was silly, and perhaps an invitation to be hurt, he couldn't resist the feelings of love that welled up within him as he drew the aroma deep into his lungs.

He loved this boy. No matter what came of the future, he would love this boy and make sure he was safe—even if that meant he was far away from their family.

Shaye stepped closer and put her hand on his arm, the simple action tender and affectionate. "I agree. I think we should call Wyatt. Maybe he can come out and we can tell him some of the situation."

He stiffened as he tried to think of a way for the local deputy to get only part of the story.

"It's okay," Zoey said, nodding. "If there's one thing I know about our cousin it's that he doesn't ask too many questions." She gave him a knowing look.

Good. He relaxed slightly. At the very least, some of the pressure was off since they had an ally in local law enforcement.

But they weren't in the clear.

"And what about the men we have tucked away here?" Chad asked.

Zoey sighed, like his question somehow annoyed her. "Don't worry about them. As of right now, they're with Jarrod and Trevor. They've had a long night." A wicked smile crossed her lips.

"Did they give us any new information?" Shaye asked, sounding the tiniest bit nervous. She was probably still worried that they'd been sent by her father.

He reached up and touched her hand, which was still resting on his arm. "They are with the Gray Wolves, right?" he asked, hoping that it would make her feel more at ease.

"They each had the brands on the inside of their arms," Zoey said. "They were made members, not just some hired guns."

Chad gave Shaye an it's-going-to-be-okay look and wrapped his arm behind her back like he could support her body as well as her soul. She gave him a weak smile, as though she was as exhausted as he was by all this.

"As for Wyatt," Zoey continued, "he's on his way. I haven't told him anything, but hopefully he won't have too many questions. If he does, well…let me be the one to handle it."

"Can I see your phone one more time?" Shaye asked, motioning for it.

Zoey frowned, clutching the phone to her chest. "Um, why?"

"Oh," Shaye said, like she must have realized what she had asked of his sister. "No, I just want to see the video of the woman again."

He looked at her. "Why? Do you think you recognized her?"

She shook her head. "I don't know. I just…

Maybe there is something in it we are missing." She sounded somewhat defeated.

Zoey lifted her phone and pulled up the video. "The more eyes, the better." She sent Shaye a smile, the first he had seen his sister give his friend since Shaye had set foot on American soil. Maybe some good had come of them both assuming he was a total jackass.

Maybe she was finally starting to warm to Shaye. He would have to be sure not to give Zoey any other reasons to relegate her back to the land of the unwelcome.

The video started, grainy at first, but quickly clearing. They watched as the woman walked up to the porch, the car seat in her hand and the diaper bag on her shoulder. She lugged the baby as though he and the seat weighed a ton, and as she moved, the diaper bag slipped down from her shoulder and she was forced to keep pushing it in place. As she put down the baby, she said something that looked like "be gone" from the movement of her lips.

She turned and walked away without looking back at the baby she had left in their care—the baby who was now sleeping peacefully in Mindy's cradling arms.

The woman slipped slightly in the snow as

she walked toward a waiting car. The video stopped.

"There has to be more," he said, wishing that it would keep going.

"All of our cameras are motion-activated," Zoey said with a slight shrug. "If she came back though, we would know it."

Shaye gasped as though she had an idea. "Wait…rewind it."

He didn't have the heart to remind her that this wasn't the nineties and they weren't watching a VHS tape, but a smile moved over his lips as he silently corrected her. He must have been spending entirely too much time with his techie sister, who would have called him out for saying something like that.

"Huh?" Zoey asked.

"Go back. Did you see she was walking toward a car? Let's zoom in, see if we can get an ID on the car." Shaye sounded excited.

Zoey skipped back in the recording. Zooming in on the car, there was little to see. It was just a normal Ford Escape.

But as he squinted, he noticed a small white sticker in the car's front window. "Look, right there," he said, pointing at the sticker. "Can you make that legible?"

Zoey clicked away, pulling and cleaning

up the sticker until they could read the word: *Alamo* in blue-and-yellow writing.

"It's a rental," Shaye said, excitement in her voice.

The rental car told them with almost complete certainty that the woman wasn't from Montana. And it gave them a place to start digging. Maybe if they could get the woman's identity nailed down, then they could figure out why she had dropped off the baby.

"I got it," Zoey said, her voice high with excitement. "Good job, Shaye, Chad. I'll go see what I can pull up from this. It shouldn't take me too long to hack into the rental car company's system and pull up their recent rental agreements."

He nodded. "I'd love to get a solid ID on this woman, as well."

"That makes two of us," Zoey said, smiling at him as she jogged down the hallway toward her office.

Mindy walked toward the door, Peanut still asleep in her arms. "I'm going to try and get him snuggled into bed so he can sleep a bit longer. If you need me, I'm in my room." She closed the door gently behind her, giving Shaye a wink as she left.

And suddenly they were alone. Very. Alone.

The room sat silent, but there was the vibration of unspoken words buzzing between them.

"I'd better go check on Trevor and Jarrod. I bet they're ready to take a break from their interrogation." Not that he had the stomach for some of the face-to-face methods his brothers used to get information from their enemies, but interrogations had be to easier than being here with Shaye.

"I'm sorry, Chad," Shaye said. "I shouldn't have—"

He shook his head, quieting her. "I know what you thought... And clearly you weren't the only one. But don't worry about it." He shrugged like it wasn't still bothering him that she thought he was capable of abandoning a baby.

"After the fistfight, and what everyone was saying?"

"What?" he said, jerking his head. He knew people assumed the worst about him, but why would anyone tell Shaye anything about him? Or had it been Kash? "Who said something?"

She looked down at her hands. "It doesn't matter who said what, I was the one who made a mistake in listening to them. I should have known what they were saying was wrong."

"I thought you knew me. My family saved

your life. And yet, you think I'm some kind of sleaze?"

She stepped toward him, but he moved away from her reach. "Chad, no… I don't think anything like that about you. I appreciate all that you and your family have done for me, but—"

"But you still thought I had fathered a baby and kept it a secret," he said, finishing her sentence.

"You can't act like it was out of the question," she countered. "You alluded to the fact that your past isn't without blemishes."

He wanted to tell her that neither was hers, but he didn't want to stoop to that level. He was mad and hurt by her suppositions, and though it would have been easier to push her away and maybe drive her from his life, he didn't want to hurt her. He just wanted to go back to the way things were before the baby came along and she had made it clear exactly what she thought of him.

"I've had women in my life, you're right," he said, but as he spoke the words it was like she had been slapped across the face.

She looked up at him with pain in her eyes.

"Damn it. That's not what I meant. I just mean—"

"It's okay, we all have a past, Chad." She

sucked in a long breath, as if she was trying to control her anger, or was it the tears that were starting to well in her eyes?

"This is all coming out wrong," he said. "I'm not really upset with you. I get how you could assume what you did. And I'm sorry that I have a reputation that would lend itself to a rush to judgment. But I'm telling you, Shaye, I don't want to keep secrets from you, of all people—"

Before he could finish his thought, there was a knock at their door. "Wyatt's here," Zoey said and stomped quickly down the hall.

"The queen is beckoning," he said, wondering if Zoey had talked about him.

Shaye gave him a look that made him question his irritation toward his sister. "I know your sister can be…*tough*."

"She hasn't been kind to you, and for that I'm sorry." He put his hand on the doorknob as he moved to go out.

"That's not entirely true," Shaye said, shaking her head. "I think she just wants the best for your family and isn't afraid to upset others to keep everyone safe. Her love is fierce."

"And so is her attitude." He could hear how angry he sounded.

"Her ferocity is something to be admired,

and she is a natural-born leader. If my father was anything like her, I think my life would have been far different."

"What do you mean?"

Shaye shook her head. "Just that he doesn't put his family first. For him, everything and everyone is fair game when it comes to getting himself ahead. My back carries many of his footprints."

He let go of the doorknob and wrapped her in his arms. As he hugged her, he drew in the scent of her lavender shampoo and the sweet smell of sleep that still lingered on her skin.

They both carried wounds deeper than time could completely heal, but that didn't mean they couldn't keep trying to learn and move past the pain inflicted by others.

"Do you accept my apology?" she asked, her breath warming his chest through the thin cotton of his T-shirt.

"I couldn't stay mad at you if I tried." And, oh, how he had tried. Pushing her away would have been so much easier than trying to make sense of what was going on inside him.

But when she was in his arms and pressed against him, she felt like she was a part of him—like just maybe she was the part of him that he'd been missing.

Chapter Thirteen

Chad and Shaye walked out of the back bedroom holding hands. As they entered the great room and Shaye looked out the front window, she let her hand slip from his. Wyatt was out in the driveway talking with Jarrod. Though it was barely a secret that they had feelings for one another, it didn't feel like the time or the place to advertise their growing relationship.

Shaye watched as Jarrod and Wyatt started walking toward the front door. Wyatt laughed, making her wonder if Jarrod had told him anything that even resembled the truth of their precarious situation.

Zoey walked out from the kitchen and flopped down on the couch. She was eating a banana and scrolling through something on her phone, almost as if it was just any other day and they weren't holding two men hostage with a stranger's baby in their midst.

It made her wonder what else this family had faced. How could they be so nonchalant when law enforcement showed up on their doorstep and so much was at stake?

Or maybe it was just that they knew they were safe with Wyatt.

Even assuming the latter, her hands were sweating and she kept rubbing them on her pants in an attempt to rid herself of her nerves. She could only imagine what would happen if Wyatt caught wind of the men in the basement. Would he arrest them all and take the men? Or would he join the family in their craziness? And if he did, would he be as kind as Mindy and Chad had been about her role in the upheaval?

And that was to say nothing of the baby.

She tried to swallow back the rest of her nervousness, but it was a losing battle.

Chad opened the door for Wyatt and Jarrod. Jarrod walked in and Wyatt took off his hat and slapped it against his leg, bumping off the snow before he stepped inside.

"This is a nice place you got yourselves here," Wyatt said, looking around the room with animal hides decorating the walls and a large river-rock fireplace at its heart. He whistled through his teeth as his gaze came to rest on the oil painting of a waterfall that sat over the hearth. "You know who this place belongs to?"

"No," Zoey said, shoving the last bit of the banana into her mouth and her phone in her pocket.

"Well, it's a nice place," Wyatt said, moving from one foot to the other as he gripped the corners of his bulletproof vest.

Chad cleared his throat as a long, awkward silence permeated through the room. "So I'm not sure exactly what my sister told you, but I'm glad you're here."

Zoey shot him a look that told him to shut up in every language. The silent edict made Shaye chuckle inwardly. *Fierce* had been an understatement. Zoey was an inspiration.

Chad stopped talking.

"Jarrod, do you want to go get the package while I talk to Wyatt here?" Zoey said, motioning her toward the back bedrooms, where the baby was sleeping.

Jarrod nodded as Zoey turned to face the deputy. "We meant to call you sooner, but hearing all that you were facing the last few days, we didn't want to burden you." Zoey sounded far softer and more supplicating than Shaye had ever heard before.

"Yes, things have been running amok here lately," Wyatt said, frowning at them.

"Though I must admit, I'm not sure I want to know exactly how you all know what's going on. By chance, you and your brothers wouldn't have any knowledge about a strange series of events that occurred at the local hardware store, would you?"

Zoey shook her head and smiled. "No idea what you're talking about," she said. "All I'd heard was that there was something going on downtown, something that involved the coroner. What happened?" She gave Wyatt a concerned look.

The woman could've been up for an award with that kind of performance.

"Apparently, one of the store's employees tripped and landed on a knife." Wyatt gave them a disbelieving look. "Though there was no evidence of foul play, and everything seems to add up to a brutal accident, if you ask me... It looked a bit *forced*." He looked over at Chad as if he could smell the guilt and fear emanating from him.

Without thinking, Shaye reached down to touch the welts on the back of her legs where she had been struck by their attacker. Did Wyatt have an idea about what had really happened?

Zoey's smile grew ever larger, and she looked more and more like the Cheshire cat.

"Was there any kind of recording, anything that could help make sense of his death?"

She sounded so innocent.

Wyatt turned to her. "Unfortunately, here in Mystery, you'll find that most everyone thinks of that as an invasion of privacy. Now and again you find somebody with cameras," he said, eyeing Zoey knowingly. "However, I find that people who run high-tech gadgets around their places always have something to hide."

"Cousin, come on. What would we have to hide from you?" Zoey laughed. "Besides, I have to disagree. In our case, we find our surveillance helps keep us safe. In fact, from what I know about your family, it may not be a bad idea for you all to get a little more security."

"You've got me there," Wyatt said with a chuckle. "Maybe our two families are more alike than I ever thought possible. And if that's the case, we'll be lucky if this town is left standing."

Shaye laughed—he was more on point than he even knew.

Zoey wrapped her arm in Wyatt's. "Now, cousin, you know that whatever we take down, we'll do our best to rebuild."

"Just make sure you don't go about taking

down my career—got it?" Wyatt said, raising an eyebrow.

Shaye wasn't sure, given the circumstances, that was a promise that Zoey could make.

Zoey walked Wyatt back toward the kitchen and she and Chad followed behind.

Chad leaned down to her ear and whispered, "I have a bad feeling that this isn't going to go as well as Zoey was hoping. We are going to need to watch for the fallout."

"Hey, trust your sister. She knows what she's about." Shaye patted him on the arm, though she had a sneaking suspicion that Chad was right.

Zoey handed Wyatt a steaming cup of coffee and motioned for him to sit down at the bar that stood at the center of the room. "Yesterday, we became the proud caregivers of a little boy."

"Oh, yeah?" Wyatt said, taking a long draw from his coffee. He glanced over at Chad, and Shaye could feel Chad grow tense. "And whose baby would this be?"

Zoey smiled and took out her phone. "Well, we are currently working on trying to find the identity of the woman who left him on our porch."

"Whoa, she *left him on your porch*?" Wyatt said, dropping the mug to the counter with a ping as it struck the glass. "What have you guys gotten yourselves into?"

"Nothing we can't get ourselves out of," Zoey said, her voice hard and unwavering and leaving no room for Wyatt to argue or question.

He shifted like he was trying to prepare himself for the weight of the situation that had been presented to him. "Do you know the baby's name? Birthdate?"

"As of right now," Zoey said, "all we know is that he's a little boy and we're guessing he's about two months old. I've been searching missing children's databases, and nothing has matched his description."

"Sounds like you've put in your paces," Wyatt said, inspecting her. "In fact, it sounds like you've done hours of research. So how long has this baby been in your care?"

Zoey's face twitched, as though she intended to say something, but checked herself. "Less than twenty-four hours."

Mindy walked out from the hallway carrying the baby and Jarrod followed after her with the baby's things. The sight made a deep, inexplicable pool of sadness within her. The feeling made her question herself. The baby wasn't theirs, so why did she feel as she did? From the very moment she had set eyes on the child, she had known that he was only going to be in their lives temporarily. And yet, watching this unfold, she couldn't help the feeling that he was being ripped out of her arms.

Glancing up, Mindy stopped as she stared at Wyatt, then back down at the baby. She looked like she was just a second away from making a run for it, baby in tow.

"Is this the dude?" Wyatt asked gently, as he walked over and pulled down the boy's blanket just enough to look on his face. As he moved the blanket, Peanut squirmed and let out a high-pitched wail, as if he was experiencing the same panic Shaye was. "Whoa, little guy, it's okay. Shh… Shh…" Wyatt said, trying to quiet the baby, but instead of quieting down, his cries became louder and more piercing.

"I think he needs a quick change and a bottle," Mindy said, her voice cracking as she headed out of the room. As she moved away, the sounds of her cooing to the baby echoed out toward them.

Jarrod stood there staring like he wasn't quite sure what he should do. He finally turned and followed his fiancée out of the room.

"I'm assuming that there's a hell of a good

reason you didn't tell me about this baby earlier," Wyatt said, glaring at all of them. "You do know, that if the baby's parents wanted, they could actually charge all of you with kidnapping if they played their cards right."

Shaye hadn't thought of that and a sickening sense of dread crept up within her. "But we didn't kidnap the baby—we have video of the mom dropping him off."

Zoey jerked and almost imperceptibly shook her head, reminding Shaye to be quiet.

"You have what?" Wyatt said, looking directly at Zoey. "I can't believe this family." He put his hands up in submission. "I'm sure you think you have your reasons for not getting me involved, but not telling me right away was stupid. It's almost like you guys are trying to get yourselves in trouble."

Once again, she couldn't disagree with the deputy. But she was right alongside the rest of the Martins, in this constant blurring between right and wrong.

"We called you now." Chad stepped between her and Wyatt, like he could somehow protect her from his cousin's fiery glare. "And we know that you're the best option that we have right now."

"What do you want me to do?" Wyatt

asked, rubbing the back of his hand over his nose in a huff.

Chad stretched his neck like he had a nervous tic. "We want you to help us keep him safe."

"I notice that you didn't say you wanted me to help find his parents," Wyatt countered.

She wasn't sure why, but somehow this family fight—even in its explosive possibilities—made it clear what a real family would do for one another. Though Wyatt had been angry about the prospect of getting this baby, and hiding it, he hadn't overtly said no. Instead, he was just angered that they'd left him out.

This family, regardless of what they could lose, were bound together by something so much more than blood.

She envied that. Moreover, she wished she could be a part of this forever.

"Of course, we want you to try and find this little boy's family, but if you don't, I know that I would be more than happy to take him under my care." As the words came from Shaye's mouth, they surprised even her. "I have the means, and I'm happy to supply you with whatever else in the way of paperwork you should need to get the adoption started."

Chad turned on his heel, staring at her as

she spoke. "Do you really mean that?" he whispered, so that only she could hear.

She nodded. For the first time since she'd gotten here, she was actually certain about something. Though she was scared witless, and though she was likely nearly the last person that anyone would entrust with the baby—given her current circumstances—she would do anything to make sure that he was protected and well-loved.

Wyatt rubbed his hands over his face, exasperated. "Whoa now. We're getting ahead of ourselves. A lot of things need to happen before we can even talk about long-term care options for this child. For now, we need to get him into the care of CPS."

"No, that's not an option." Zoey sounded angry at the proposition. "We're not putting this kid in some foster home while your department comes to the same dead ends I've been facing. While I know that there are some great foster-home options out there, there are also some that I wouldn't wish upon my worst enemies. If you're gonna stick him in some hellhole, I am not giving you this baby. It may be a little bit dangerous here, but it's better than whatever he might face out there."

Shaye walked over and stood at Zoey's side, making a show of a united front.

Wyatt sank down, resting on the sofa as he dropped his head into his hands.

"There has to be another option. If not, we can keep working to figure out who the baby's biological parents are, and maybe even get his name." Zoey crossed her arms over her chest. "If I find something I don't like or if I can't get the information I need, I'm more than capable of getting my hands on the appropriate paperwork to make it seem like he was born into this family."

Wyatt looked up at her. "If you're hellbent on breaking the law, why did you call me here? Did you want some moral support, someone to tell you that it was okay to steal a baby just because someone left him on your porch? We don't understand or know the circumstances behind this baby's arrival at the ranch, but I'm more than certain that we need to follow the law with this one." Wyatt's hands flew around as he spoke. "It can't just be circumstantial that this baby randomly arrives on your doorstep the day a man turns up dead by some freak accident and I also get reports of a high-speed chase on the highway. You guys are up to something, and I know it. You're lucky you're family, or I would be dragging all of your butts to jail."

She had heard the expression "so angry a person could spit" but until now she hadn't experienced a moment that quite fit that idiom. Yet as she watched Wyatt's face redden with anger and little bits of spittle fly from his lips, she finally understood.

But she couldn't be upset with him for his reaction. He was a man with honor, a man bound by the oath of his office to do what was right…a man who cared about this nameless baby and his welfare just as much as they did, and he'd only met the child for a few seconds.

Shaye walked around Chad and sat down beside Wyatt on the sofa, hoping against all hope that she could do something to help instead of further strain the situation. "Wyatt, we all understand how you're feeling. And we are sorry for putting you in such a terrible position. If we didn't feel as though it was absolutely necessary, we wouldn't have called you here."

Zoey nodded, but she still appeared reticent at Shaye's intrusion into her plan. "And just so you know, Wyatt, while we aren't here to cause trouble, we are hoping to stay off the radar."

"Does that mean what I think it does?" Wyatt asked, giving Zoey a tired look.

"It means that if you don't want to put your career in jeopardy, it is best if you don't ask too many questions. And we will do our best to keep you out of our trouble," Zoey said.

Wyatt swore under his breath.

Shaye dropped her hands into a prayer position between her knees as she turned toward him, hoping that he would see that she was speaking to him in all earnestness. "For now, there has to be something you can do with this child. Something that will ensure his safety until the danger sweeping through this community is resolved."

A lump swelled in her throat as she thought about the truth she had just danced around. The *community* wasn't the problem nearly as much as *she* was.

"There is another option," Wyatt said, but his face paled slightly as he spoke. "My mother, Eloise Fitzgerald, has always had a soft spot for taking in kids who are in need. She would box my ears if she heard I had gone against you guys and put this baby in foster care."

"Yes, and Anya will love having him over there. She loves babies," Zoey said, supporting her with a hand on her shoulder. "And if you need to write up a report or something, you can say we're working as consultants on the case, helping to find the child's parents. And maybe, when things cool down, we could come and see him. Help your mom out, or whatever you need."

"Whoa, I'm not putting any of this in writing," Wyatt said, shaking his head. "If I do, I'll be out on my ass. I've been walking a fine line at the department for the last year or two. If they find out I didn't follow the departmental policy on this one… Well, we're not going to talk about what would happen."

Chad sighed. "Wyatt, you can't put your job at risk for us. That's not right, either."

Zoey shot him a look, but Shaye couldn't disagree with him.

Wyatt stood up and looked down the hall in the direction Mindy and Jarrod had fled with the child, then turned back. "The way I see it, none of this discussion ever happened. For now, I'll take him over to my mom's place. He can stay there for a bit, but I want you to look into the whereabouts of this boy's family. When you find them, you tell me."

"And if we don't?" Shaye asked, a sliver of hope curling around her dreams of having a child.

Wyatt looked at her with a deadly seriousness. "I don't advocate breakin' any laws just so you all can play house. When it comes to this boy, we are going to do what's best."

As Wyatt disappeared down the hall, so did her hope and dreams of a future with this baby.

Chapter Fourteen

Holy crap, Shaye had to have lost her mind. He couldn't believe that she'd actually offered to adopt the baby. With everything going on, he hadn't really considered the long-term prospects of the child. But she must've put all kinds of thought into it. And if she had, then why hadn't she talked to him about it? Which brought him back to the place where he questioned what exactly was going on between them.

There was no doubt in his mind that she had feelings for him and vice versa, but now he questioned her intentions. There was no way that he would have agreed to something so life-changing without consulting her.

Clearly, he must've been reading more into the situation and what was there.

They spent the rest of the day sifting through online records and photo banks and any lead that they thought could provide them with more information. Surprisingly, the car-rental website had proved more of a hassle than Zoey had anticipated, but she let out a loud whoop when she finally made it past their safeguards and opened up access to their servers.

"I'm in," Zoey said, showing them all her tablet's screen like it was a major award.

Shaye was sitting beside him on the sofa, but since Wyatt had left with Peanut, they had barely said a word to one another. He glanced over at her, hoping that this little bit of good news would help raise her spirits, but she seemed unchanged.

He stuffed his phone in his pocket, frustrated both with his lack of headway and his inability to say the words that needed to be said to Shaye. Part of him wished he could go back in time and tell Zoey that they would keep the baby and that Wyatt needed to stay away, but it was too late now.

They sat in silence, nervously watching as Zoey worked to nail down the identity of the boy's guardian, until he couldn't take the silence another moment. He couldn't sit here idly and watch—he had to move.

He got up off the couch, went to the kitchen and decided to make himself and the rest of the family tuna salad for lunch. As he stumbled around the kitchen, looking through the drawers for spoons and knives, the door opened and Shaye came inside.

He stopped as the door closed behind her, and they stood staring at one another. It was as if neither of them knew exactly what to say, or how to proceed.

"Hungry?" he asked, finally breaking the tense silence between them.

She nodded, walked to the fridge and pulled out a bottle of sparkling water. "Can I help you do something?"

So this was how it was going to be—they were both going to delicately dance around all the things they were thinking and feeling instead of actually heading them off. He didn't mind the footwork involved in this dance. He was nearly an expert in avoiding everything that involved actual emotions. He'd been practicing this his whole life, and until recently, doing a damn good job of it… That was, until she had reappeared in his life.

Or maybe now things could go back to the way they had been—comfortable and completely repressed.

He handed her a sharp knife and a jar of pickles. Without a word, she pulled out a pickle and started slicing away.

As they worked in silence, their bodies

seem to take on each other's rhythm, as if they were also weaving around the invisible bombs of stress and trauma that littered the space between them. As they moved, he couldn't deny that there was something beautiful about it—the way they could eloquently avoid the other's emotional triggers, yet still want to be so physically close. It was as if their hearts yearned to speak the words that their mouths refused.

He wished that being with her was easy and carefree—if it had been, perhaps they would be chatting away, dreaming of their futures together. He could almost envision what it would be like had everything been less stressful. By now perhaps they would've been sharing a bed and whispering their secrets. She could have been ready to move forward, and he the same.

At least they were stuck in this weird emotional place, and a life full of drama, together. He could think of no one he would rather be with.

He shook the thoughts from his head as he pulled out two slices of bread from the bag and rested them on the cutting board near Shaye.

Yes, repression was far easier than having to feel the sparks in his fingertips when he gently brushed against Shaye's arm, or the way he felt when he leaned in so close to her that he could smell the sweet scent of lavender on her hair. Everything about her drew him in. It was like she was his own personal drug—and being with her, or contemplating being with her, was nearly as dangerous.

"What's that for?" she asked, pointing her knife toward the bread.

"Gonna make tuna sandwiches for the crew," he said, like the answer was obvious.

"Okay…" She sounded a tad confused by the meal, but continued chopping until she had a nice little stack of pickles.

"Haven't you had a tuna-salad sandwich before?" He gave her a disapproving look.

"I've had tuna, and sandwiches, but not a tuna sandwich." She gave him a little grin, and some of the tension he was feeling lifted. He was sure she hadn't meant to smile, but it made him feel better nonetheless. More than anything, it gave him hope that with enough time they could get past the initial shock of handing over the baby.

She had to have known it was the right thing to do. Maybe that was why she was finally coming around.

She walked over to the fridge and opened the door, peering inside. "Where's the tuna?"

"Here, we only have the best—the kind in a can. I know, so much swankier than what you are used to," he said, walking over to the pantry and pulling out a can of Chicken of the Sea.

She covered her mouth as she gave a little squeak of a laugh. "Oh, yeah… I…"

"Have you seen tuna in a can before?"

"Only at the store," she admitted, looking even more chagrined.

"Dang, lady, you are in for a real treat. There's *tuna* and then there is *tuna*," he said, slapping down a couple of cans on the counter like they were the gold standard for lunch boxes everywhere.

"Has anyone ever told you that there is likely something really wrong with you?"

He winked at her in a sexy, sideways glance. "Just because I love a good sandwich."

"That among many other things. Namely, that you can't take anything too seriously."

That wasn't entirely true, but he was relieved to have her think such a thing of him. Taking anything too seriously was just a quicker way to age oneself.

As he set about putting together the ingredients, it felt good to be setting around the kitchen, puttering away and getting the opportunity to do something that was just *normal.*

He was really going to have to focus on enjoying the small things in life. If they kept coming under attack it was hard to say how many more of these tiny diamonds of time would come his way.

He handed Shaye a sandwich and she daintily picked at the crust, pulling it off and setting it on a napkin before taking on the food.

In truth, tuna salad was far from his favorite lunch, but it was the only thing that had come to mind when he had set foot in the kitchen, but now it was too late to tell her that it wasn't the best American food out there. Now, hot dogs…that was another story entirely.

She took a tentative bite, and she nodded as she took another bite. As she looked up from her sandwich, she gave him a thumbs-up. "This is good," she said, her words muffled as she spoke with her mouth full.

It was good to see her being less than perfect. And as silly as it was, it made him like her more…and the thought made him realize that every second he spent with her, he liked her more. Given time, he could only imagine what he would feel for her in five, ten or even twenty years.

From a single second to twenty years, being with her was one journey that he wanted to take.

He ate a sandwich, downing it with a glass of milk, and then made a few more. After putting some veggies beside the sandwiches on the platter, they carried it out to the living room. Jarrod was sitting with Mindy and whispering. They both looked up and stopped talking as he walked into the room, making Chad wonder what they had been talking about.

He set the plate on the table in front of the couch. "We thought you guys might be needing a little bite."

Jarrod reached over, grabbed a sandwich and started stuffing it in his mouth as he looked over at Zoey, like she was the only one who could answer any questions.

Zoey didn't even look up, and seemed completely unaware that anyone else was even in the room.

"So she hasn't found anything yet?" Shaye asked Jarrod, motioning in Zoey's direction.

Jarrod shook his head, bread crumbs tumbling from his mouth.

Mindy opened a box. Inside was a stack of black T-shirts. She threw each one of them a shirt, and as Chad caught his, he felt its heaviness. He twisted the fabric in his fingers. "Is this one of your—"

"Yep, it's from our new line of bulletproof clothing for Monster Wear." Mindy nodded and set a shirt beside Zoey, who was so focused she didn't even budge. "We are working on creating an even lighter, more breathable fabric at our manufacturing plant in Sweden. This is one of our new prototypes. It's been field-tested and I recommend we all start wearing them."

Though he completely understood Mindy's reason for giving them new gear, it made their position seem even more vulnerable. He gave her a nod of thanks and threw the shirt over his arm.

Mindy frowned. "It's important that we all remain as protected as we can. It would look ridiculous if one of us got shot when our family specializes in tactical gear and security and we can't even keep ourselves safe."

He knew she wasn't just concerned about business. Mindy was scared.

Jarrod patted her leg, but Mindy straightened her back, putting on a show of resolve—something Chad knew all too much about.

Poorly masked fear slithered around the room. There was no way Chad could sit there, waiting and watching, biding time until they found the answers they were looking for.

"Is there a gym in this house anywhere?" he asked, thinking about taking a run in order to work off some of his excess nervous energy.

Mindy pointed toward the stairs. "Downstairs. It's on the west end of the hall. I took a peek in there, looks nice."

"Cool," he said. He took Shaye's hand and led her toward the stairs. Shaye didn't protest and instead seemed relieved that he was helping her to escape.

At the bottom of the stairs, to their right, was the hallway that led to the panic room where they were keeping the hostages. From where they stood, he could make out the sounds of Trevor's voice coming out from behind the room's open door. He was saying something about having plenty of time on his hands.

Trevor's words were false. The one thing they didn't seem to have much of was time. With each passing second, they were moving closer and closer to being found, attacked and perhaps even killed.

Yes, he definitely needed to get in a run. Maybe it would help him get his head right. Being pessimistic at a time like this was the last thing that anyone needed. Over the years he'd had it drilled into him that one thing was true above all others—what he thought, and therefore believed, always became reality.

They would come through this fine. Everything would be fine, he tried to tell himself, but the sounds of his inner voice sounded just as false as Trevor's words.

The gym was bigger than he had anticipated, and it appeared as though the owners had every piece of equipment he could imagine. As nice and as fancy as this place looked, in reality he probably only knew how to use about five of the pieces. He'd grown accustomed to makeshift gyms, products of war zones. More than once he had resorted to lifting jugs filled with sand and running on cart paths in order to get in a workout. In fact, he probably spent more time working out in those kinds of conditions than he had in a place like this.

As he flipped on the lights, the place was filled with brightness, thanks to the mirrors that lined the walls. It was purely a gym-rat thing to want to stand there and watch yourself get all sweaty. Or maybe it wasn't gym-rat, but rather a narcissistic thing. He understood the need to know whether or not a person was using the proper techniques, but really…it was too much. He preferred sand and grit any day.

Shaye walked by him and he could hear her suck in a long breath. "Wow, I thought the gym at the palace was nice, but this is a whole different level."

"So you work out a lot?" If he didn't have to work out for his job, he wasn't sure that he would work out as much as he did. It was so much easier to eat Cheetos and watch HGTV

He closed the door behind them, locking it so he didn't have to worry about any unwanted guests.

She looked at him with the raise of an eyebrow. "What do you think?"

No, he had totally just walked into that one. That was stupid. He made a show of looking her up and down, assessing her, even though he knew that she was perfect. He had spent more than his fair share of time watching her curves as she walked, and the graceful way her body moved. By most standards, she might have been a little bit on the heavy side, but a person's weight was ever-changing, so to base attraction on such a fickle thing was tasteless and shallow. All that really mattered was that she felt happy with the woman she was—there was nothing more attractive than confidence.

He put down the shirt Mindy had given him and walked over to Shaye. They were safe here. At least, one of them was.

A fire rippled up from deep in his belly as Shaye gave him a playful smile.

"You know, in order for me to get a really good idea of what I think, I'm going to need to give you a closer inspection," he said, putting his hands on her waist.

She gave him a look of surprise, like she hadn't been expecting him to play along. "The last time I checked, looking was done with your eyes not with your hands." She stepped back, giving him a cheeky grin.

"Then let's pretend I'm blind," he teased, reaching out for her again.

She gave a belly laugh, and looked down at his extended hands before stepping into his grasp. "I think it's only fair if I get to give you a good once-over, as well," she said in a soft voice, as she ran her hands down the muscles of his chest.

He had wanted to get in a good and sweaty workout, but he hadn't been expecting anything like this—not even in his wildest dreams.

She traced her finger down the line of his shirt. "I hear the best kind of workouts are the ones that you do without a shirt," she said in a serious-sounding voice.

"Is that right?" he asked, but the last thing he wanted to do was argue.

His breath caught in his throat as her fingers drifted over his naked skin, tracing the fine hairs on his chest and his nipples. He had wanted her to touch him like this since… well, forever.

She leaned into him and ran her lips over the places her fingers had caressed. Her hot breath made goose bumps rise on his skin. Yes. He wanted this. He wanted her. He wanted it all.

He reached up and pushed her hair back from her face so he could watch her as she kissed him. She glanced up at him as she pulled his nipple into her mouth and traced her teeth against it, making it spark to life with this little taste of agony.

As she kissed him, his body responded, pressing almost painfully against the harsh fabric of his tac pants. He throbbed as she moved to his other nipple and pushed his shirt from his shoulders.

Her fingers trailed downward, finding the waist of his pants, but she stopped there and let her fingers linger.

It had been so long since he had been

touched the way that she was touching him that he was forced to look away, at the awful mirrors. But they were no help. Instead, surrounding him was her—everywhere and from every angle. He was forced to shut his eyes, but that too only intensified the sensations of her lips on his skin.

SHAYE LOOKED UP at him as he gently stepped back from her grasp. What was happening? Didn't he like what she was doing to him?

Licking the flavor of his sweat from her lips, she smiled. Though she wasn't sure she wanted to know the answer—out of fear that he was overthinking everything that was happening between them—she asked, "What's wrong?" She paused for a moment. "Is it okay that I'm kissing you?"

He took her hands in his. As she stood upright, he used their entwined hands to move a piece of hair from her face—it was almost as though he feared letting her go even for a second, and that little gesture softened the blow of his retreat.

"It's more than okay," he said, sounding breathless. "I love that you are kissing me."

"Then why do you want me to stop?" she asked, the hurt flecking her voice.

"Oh, I don't. I just…" He glanced down and then his cheeks reddened.

"Oh," she said, checking her giggle before it could escape her. She didn't want him to think she was laughing at him, not at all… If anything, she was thrilled that she could elicit such a strong response. "We can take things a bit slower."

He ran his hand over the back of his neck. "Yeah, I'm sorry… You just caught me a bit off-guard. I was expecting a run," he said, motioning in the direction of the treadmills.

"We can still use the treadmill if you want." She gave him a toying glance.

Had he really brought her down here just to work out? The way he had sounded in the kitchen with her, he'd been so playful and charming, it hadn't occurred to her that it had been anything other than a ploy for them to be alone. Had it just been wishful thinking on her part?

Ever since they had shared the kiss, she had been envisioning something more with him, and then chastising herself. But standing here, now, her body aching for him to draw nearer to her again, she didn't want to over-think it. She just wanted him to kiss her as she had kissed him, to make him beg her for release…and sate her every desire.

If hellfire was going to rain down on them, the least she could do was take each day as it came—and that meant finally listening to the desire that careened through her, awakening every part of her body. This was their moment. Alone. Together. And it was their time to give in to their needs.

There was no going back. Body and soul, she was ready to give herself to him.

She moved closer to him, wrapping her arms around his neck as he pulled her against his awakened body.

"I want you, Shaye. I've wanted you for so long," he whispered, closing his eyes and dropping his head to hers so their foreheads touched. "You are the reason I look forward to waking up each morning. And when you came here, to me... I've never been happier."

She was shocked to hear him speak so candidly. Chad had never opened up like this to her before. Her already softened heart melted completely.

Yes. This.

She leaned up and kissed him, taking in the dill flavor of his lips.

"Mmm, pickles," she said, without taking her lips from his.

"I was thinking the same thing," he said with a laugh. "I could eat you up."

"Here's hoping," she said, pulling out of his arms and moving coyly away from him. She started to jog, beckoning him to the chase. "But I'm not an easy girl to have. If you want me, you have to catch me first."

He threw his head back in a laugh, giving her a moment to put distance between them before he gave chase.

He looked at her with hunger in his eyes, and she was certain that the moment he caught her, there would be no time for second thoughts or removal of nonvital clothes. She loved that primal yearning.

For a moment, she was the master and he was her plaything...but that control wouldn't last for long.

She stepped behind a big black machine with long armlike attachments. Moving fast, she stripped off her pants, exposing her lacy purple-and-black panties, and she threw them into the middle of the room. "How badly do you want me?"

He grumbled, the sound nearly a growl as he stepped toward her. As he reached her pants, he stopped and removed his shirt and dropped it on top.

His muscles...oh, his muscles. He had a faint line of blond hair that ran over his pecks and down past his navel, then disappeared beneath the waistband of his pants. His skin was tan, but markedly lighter than hers—his was closer to the color of honey. She licked her lips at the thought of his salty kiss and the sweet flavor of his nipples as she had sucked them into her mouth.

She darted down the aisle, moving three rows back. He grumbled again, the sound more fervent with desire. Pulling off her plum-colored top, she threw it away from the machine, and as she moved her warm skin brushed against the cold black metal, making her gasp.

Until now, she hadn't realized how electrified her senses had become after being charged by his touch...and his kiss.

He stopped moving as she stepped out from behind the machine in only her bra and panties. She covered her body with one arm and raised her other hand to her lips, making a sexy pose.

Even from a few feet away, she could hear him suck in his breath.

Good. Exactly the reaction I wanted.

"Shaye... My... You..." he said, stumbling over his words. "You are so freaking beautiful."

She smiled over at him, sliding behind the last machine—the treadmill—that sat nearest the wall. He moved slowly toward her, like she was a spooked filly and any moment she could bolt. But as he neared, she only stepped back until she was nearly touching the mirrored wall behind her.

He reached up, tracing the edge of her bra with the littlest bit of his fingertip. Her skin flamed as he barely grazed her skin. Her body quaked as he took her fullness into the cup of his hand and he kissed her. He pressed against her, bumping her warm, nearly naked body up against the cold mirror. She gasped at the chill and the fire of his touch and the power of his kiss.

He reached down and touched her over the thin fabric of her panties, running circles over the fabric with his fingers until she nearly couldn't stand.

"Please…" It was all she could think…or say.

He scooped her up and she wrapped her legs around him. Opening up only his zipper, he pushed aside her panties and teased himself into her, slowly at first. As she opened to him, he drove deeper and deeper inside her.

They moved together, finding a natural rhythm. The mirror on the wall behind her bumped as they made love and the sound only made her more turned-on. This was their symphony, the cadence of their union.

Though she wasn't ready, her body betrayed her with a quiver. She exploded around him, collapsing against his body as she gave into the all-powerful ecstasy of their love.

Chapter Fifteen

She lay on the treadmill, looking up at him. Her face was covered in a thin sheen of sweat and she was breathing hard.

"I didn't know my body could do that," she said, tracing her fingers over the dark hair a few inches below her belly button.

He sat up on his elbow beside her. "I'm glad we can explore new worlds together," he said, leaning down and kissing the skin of her breast.

Three times. It was a new record for him pleasing a woman, but he wasn't about to admit that to her. As he looked down on her beautiful, naked body, he considered going for number four, but his body ached in all the wrong ways.

If he was going to have her again, he would need time to recover and likely so would she. Besides, some things were even better the second time—or the fourth.

He stood up, his knees and hips spent from their adventure. Holding out his hand, he helped her to standing and she staggered a bit.

"I'm not going to lie," she said "I'm glad to get off the belt." She turned to look at herself in the mirror. Her back and down her round butt was speckled with the waffle pattern of the treadmill's belt.

"Oh, babe, I'm sorry." He ran his hand down the texture of her back.

She gave him a wide smile. "Don't worry, I'm not. Besides, that was exactly the work-out that I needed."

He laughed, the sound reverberating throughout the mirrored room.

"And," she said, pointing at the mirror behind him, "I had one heck of a view. When I get my own house, I'm going to have to look in to a room just like this."

"But at least with a couch," he said, pointing down at his knees. They were angry and raw thanks to the nonstick floor that ran throughout the room.

"Oh, you think you would be invited to my house?" she teased.

"Well, I doubt that anyone can please you like I do," he said, more than aware that what they had just done was the best sexual experience in his entire life. He could happily live and die between her thighs.

She gave him a satisfied smile. "You know, if we had a bit more time I would kiss those knees for you, but I think it may lead to number four. I'm not sure my body could take any more. I fear that I would never be able to walk again."

"I would be more than happy to carry you around like the princess you are," he said, giving her buns a little squeeze that made her squeal.

She turned away from him and grabbed her panties and bra, then started to get dressed. "As tempting as that is, I think we probably need to check in with your family and see if anyone has found out anything about the baby yet. I'm worried about him."

And just like that, the lust-filled spell that had come over him disappeared and he was swept back into the gaping maw of reality.

As she slipped on the shirt that Mindy had given her, she looked over at him. "It's going to be okay, Chad. I know you're worried, too."

She must have seen the concern wash over him. "I just want to go back to a normal *life*—stop hiding out. You know what I mean?"

Though they had just spent the last hours

making love in several positions, his words seemed to feel almost as intimate. He hadn't really *talked* in a long time.

She picked up his clothes and walked over to him. "Lift up your arms," she said, slipping on the tac T-shirt as she spoke. "I know this may sound cynical, but this—all *this* upheaval is life. It may not be for everyone, but it's ours. And as crazy and manic as it is, for me it's easy to lose sight of what is important and the things that really matter. But one thing I've come to love about you is that you always put the focus on your family and your group."

She must have meant *love* in the platonic sense, but as she spoke, he tried to not overanalyze.

"We try, but we have our issues."

"What family doesn't?" She gave him a look that made it clear she was talking about her own.

She picked up his pants and helped him to step into them. It felt strange, her helping him dress, but at the same time, he loved it—the closeness. There was a sense of intimacy in her actions that made his heart burn in his chest. Whether she meant platonic or not, he loved her with a ferocity he had never known before.

He reached down and zipped his pants, but as he did his hand brushed against hers. He entwined his fingers with hers and pulled her hands behind his back, and then he took her in his arms. "Shaye," he said, taking in the soft sweet scent of sweat wafting up from her hair. "I want you to know… I care for my family, and I always will be there for them. But you are even more important to me."

She pulled him tighter and buried her face in his chest, and though she said nothing he could feel that she felt the same.

"Shaye, I—"

There was a knock on the door. Stopping him just as he was about to say the one word he feared above all others—love.

Son of a…

She pulled herself from his arms, almost as if she feared that someone would see them. His arms had never been emptier.

"What's up?" he asked, sounding annoyed even to his own ears. He grabbed his flannel and slipped it on over his T-shirt as he walked toward the door.

The place where Shaye had buried her face was still warm.

"I need a break," Trevor said, his voice sounding worn and ragged as he spoke.

Chad rushed to the door and flung it open.

Trevor's eyes were dark, and as tired as he had sounded, he looked a thousand times worse. His hair was disheveled and there was a line of white, dried sweat around the neck of his dark shirt.

"What's up?" he asked.

Trevor motioned for them to follow him. They rushed down the hall toward the panic room. The door stood open, and as they approached, he recognized the two men who had followed them in the Suburban. The man nearest to him, the one with red hair, looked to be asleep with his chin pressed down against his chest while the other man, who had a wide nose and prognathic mouth, sneered at them as they walked in. He was missing his two front teeth, and the gums that had once held them were swollen and bruised. The room stank of dirty bodies and bile, and the stench assaulted his senses.

"Not surprised you can't handle us," the man slurred at Trevor. "They told me that your clan was nothing but a bunch of pansies." He spat a mouthful of blood on the floor.

Shaye sucked in a breath behind Chad, drawing his attention. Taking her gently by the arm, he walked out of the room as he gave Trevor a look of warning.

She was tough and had seen worse, but she didn't need to get wrapped up in what could be a bloody interrogation. He glanced back at the redheaded man. He couldn't tell whether he was dead or alive.

His thoughts moved to Trish. Seeing pictures of her lying dead on the warehouse floor. She looked at peace as the life had leaked out of her body and poured on the concrete. A lump formed in his throat.

There was so much death in his life. Around every turn, someone died. And it wasn't just him, but everyone in his family. It was like anyone who came into their lives was doomed to a rapid and violent death.

Shaye was watching him, and as she blinked, his thoughts flashed to her lying on the floor instead of Trish.

He wasn't sure if it was some kind of premonition or just his own fears that put the image in his mind, but he couldn't risk it. He wouldn't be able to live with himself if he lost the woman he loved.

It was better if she got the hell out of this wretched place. It would break him to be apart from her, but for her own well-being he had to do what was right. He loved her. And loving someone meant putting their needs before his own.

Trevor gently closed the door behind them as Chad took Shaye into the hall and out of the room.

As much as he loved her, and because he loved her, this had to be done.

"Shaye—" he began.

"Don't worry about that," she said, interrupting him. "I have seen worse."

This wasn't about what she had and hadn't experienced in her life. This was about what he didn't want her to ever experience again.

"Shaye," he said, looking down at the place on her arm where he was touching her. He stared at the dark hair on her arms. It was the same shade as that on her head but a touch lighter than what he had just seen in the gym—hair he would probably never see again. "I think you should go back to your father."

"What?" she sounded flabbergasted, and she pulled her arm from his grasp and took two large steps away from him. "After what we just did, I…" She threw her hands up in the air. "You are being ridiculous."

Though he was sure that he appeared that way, he knew he wasn't. It was ripping out his heart to say the words he had to say to her. Undoubtedly, when she left, his entire being would shrivel away to nothing, but he had to protect her in the only way he knew how—by pushing her away.

If she stayed here, it was really only a matter of time until she got hurt…or killed.

He could feel time and their enemies pressing down on him, and loving her meant putting her before anything and everyone else, even himself.

"Your father sent a man to get you because he knows how close you are to getting hurt because of me."

"And you think this, what you are saying to me right now, doesn't hurt?"

"I'm trying to do what's best." He jabbed his finger toward the closed door behind him. "These men are just two of hundreds who want to kill me…my family. No doubt, there are teams of people looking for these guys or working for the same people. You and I both know that no matter where I go, or what I do, my shelf life is going to be limited."

"That's a lie and you know it. We are safe here." But as she spoke there was a certain amount of acknowledgment in her tone that told him that she knew he was right.

"Go home, Shaye. Your father and his army are far more capable of keeping you safe right now."

"My father… I would rather die here then

spend another second with that man. I wrote him off. He's dead to me." She pressed her back against the wall and he could see tears in her eyes. "He wants to kill…" She paused, unable to continue.

It pained him to make her feel like this, but he loved her. He loved her with his entire being. He had to do what needed to be done.

At least that is what he had to tell himself to get through this.

Once she was gone, he could break down, but for now he had to be tough. He had to get her to go—even if that meant lying to her. This was for her own good.

"Shaye, you know I think you are amazing. And I had one hell of a good time in the gym. But while we were together…well, I realized that I don't think we're relationship material." The lie burned like acid on his tongue.

Her hand came out of nowhere as she slapped him. As badly as his face stung, the burn wasn't nearly as bad as the scorch in his soul. No matter how much she hated him, he hated himself more.

Anger flashed in her eyes. "I can't believe that you are doing this to me. Kash told me you just keep women around for a booty call. I didn't believe him, but now I know, you really are that kind of man."

Chapter Sixteen

That was it, she didn't understand men. At all. Ever.

He had used her and then thrown her out of his house. What kind of man did such a thing?

Easy. Chad Martin.

If STEALTH had a cruelty division, he would be their captain. And she would be his jester.

She had been so stupid for coming here.

As she raced away from him, Shaye tried to control her tears. She was so mad. Mad at him for what he had said and done, and mad at herself for her tears. She bit her lip, drawing blood, as she tried to keep her emotions in check.

He couldn't see her cry.

He couldn't see how much he had hurt her. If he did, he would know that she loved him. And she absolutely could not, under any circumstances, love that man.

Hate, loathe and despise, yes…but love…

And yet, as she rounded the corner to ascend the stairs, she wanted to look back at him. To look at his face one more time to see if he had really meant what he had said to her.

As he had spoken, he had looked like a broken man, his head down low and his back hunched. His eyes had been dark and his face haggard, a stark contrast to just moments before when he had been looking down on her face, their eyes connecting as their bodies explored the edges of overwhelming ecstasy.

He had shifted so suddenly, so unexpectedly.

She had to have missed something, something that triggered his words.

But even if she understood why, it wouldn't make the blow any easier to take.

Screw him.

She took the stairs two at a time. As she turned the corner toward the great room, her foot struck the baby's diaper bag that was sitting on the floor. Jarrod must have forgotten to give it to Wyatt.

The baby. The hostages. The attacks.

Ugh.

She picked up the bag and took a long series of breaths, part of her hoping to hear

Chad's footsteps on the stairs as he chased after her, but there was nothing.

She didn't need him in her life, anyway.

But even as the thought floated through her mind, she knew it was a lie. She loved Chad. She was furious with him, but damn it, she loved him.

No. No. You don't, she reminded herself.

Running the back of her hand over her cheeks, checking to make sure that nothing would give her away, she entered the room where Zoey was still puttering away. Jarrod and Mindy were sitting on the couch with each other, holding hands as they looked at something on their phones.

They didn't even look up as she came into the room and made her way toward the front door. But as she pulled the door open, Zoey finally seemed to notice her.

"What are you doing?" Zoey asked, her voice raspy from not being used.

"We forgot to give Wyatt the diaper bag. I think they're going to need it for Peanut," she said, lifting the bag like it was evidence.

Zoey sighed. "Just leave it by the couch. I'll just text him to stop by when he can and pick it up. We're on lockdown. And I'm starting to get reports of possible members of Gray Wolves arriving at the airport."

She didn't care what happened to her if she left this ranch. Staying here was out of the question. "The baby's formula, diapers, everything—they're going to need them," she said, some of her strength leeching from her as she repeated the feeble excuse to leave. Instead of continuing to argue, she dropped the bag onto the floor.

Zoey looked up at her and when their eyes met, Shaye looked away, fearing that Zoey would be able to see all the hurt she was feeling.

"What happened?" Zoey asked, putting down her tablet and getting up off the couch. "Where's Chad?" She sounded concerned.

"He's fine, just downstairs with Trevor. They're working on getting answers." As she spoke, the image of the man with no teeth popped into her mind. Even with teeth the man would have been terrifying, but without them he looked like something out of a horror movie…like the man standing in the shadows holding the butcher knife.

A chill ran down her spine.

In her world, every shadow held danger—even the shadows in which she was standing.

"I'll just run this over. No one knows my rental car," Shaye continued, pulling open the door and stepping out onto the porch.

The cold made her nostrils burn as she took in a deep breath. The subtle pain was refreshing—physical pain was always easier to handle than the emotional kind.

"Shaye, stop. If you go, I can't let you come back." Zoey gave her a pained expression, like she really didn't want her to leave. "You could lead our enemies straight to us. We can't risk it."

The change in Zoey's attitude toward her didn't fail to register. How could things with Zoey have shifted so dramatically?

What was up with this family? Why did everything with them have to be so complicated?

But then, who was she to complain about complicated?

"I know." As she spoke, Shaye closed the door behind her, blocking out all that was the Martins.

Digging her keys out of her pocket, she let the tears finally fall. They blurred her vision as she walked down the steps and out to the driveway, where her rental car waited.

She had no idea where she would go—all she knew was that she had to get out of here.

She couldn't stand spending one more second this close to Chad. Even from here, she could feel the pull, the inexplicable magnetism that made her want to go running to him—they could yell and scream, curse and flail, but maybe if she went back, they could make this right. He could explain to her why he had attacked her with the one weapon he knew would hurt her the most.

Yes, Chad was the worst kind of man.

Angrily, she wiped away the tears. She hit Unlock on her car fob and opened the door.

As she moved to step into the car, a hand grabbed her from behind. A scream rippled through the air, but it was cut short by a hand over her mouth. "Shut up," a man growled in her ear. "If you want to live, you need to shut the hell up."

She tried to pull at the man's hands, to uncover her mouth and catch a glimpse of whoever was holding her, but as she scratched at his skin his grip on her only tightened. She dug her fingernails into his flesh until she could feel the skin give way and a wet, sticky blood ooze over her fingers.

"You little bitch," he said, his voice flecked with what sounded like a Turkish accent. "You're lucky your father wants you alive, or you would already be dead." He leaned in and took a long sniff of her hair, making her squirm with disgust.

She struggled harder, her body flailing in the man's grip, and as she moved to kick, another set of hands grabbed her ankles. The men held her so tightly that even though she tried to struggle, she could barely move.

They lifted her into the back of her car, and as they moved, she silently prayed that someone in the house had heard her scream. A dark-haired man climbed into the back of her car. He had a long goatee, and his face was the color of someone who spent hours in the sun. He pulled out some rope and tied her ankles, then, with a tight yank, he wrenched her arms behind her back and hog-tied her. They slapped a piece of black tape over her mouth. She tried to bite at it and push at it with her tongue, but it was stuck firmly to her skin.

Her heart raced in her chest. They weren't sent her to kill her…but that didn't mean they couldn't beat her. And what about her friends? They were inside, seemingly totally unaware of what was happening out here.

There had been men posted around the house, keeping guard for the family, but where were they now?

And how had these men found her? No one knew where she and the Martins were hiding except Wyatt. Had he told someone where they could be found?

If she saw her father again, she was going

to kill him herself for getting her into this situation.

Her hatred for the man who had fathered her roiled in her, threatening to make her explode. Until now, she hadn't thought it possible to hate someone as much as she hated him.

If Chad got hurt because of her father…

A sob rattled through her, escaping through her nose.

This couldn't be happening again. He had already killed Raj. He and his men couldn't take Chad, too.

She rubbed her face on the seat of the car, hoping to peel back a corner of the tape. If she could yell, maybe the Martins would stand a chance. They had done so much for her, taking her in and helping her escape her father…and yet she had repaid their kindnesses by bringing their enemies straight to their doorstep.

She rubbed harder until her skin burned and she was sure that she had rubbed her face raw.

She had been so foolish to walk out, to think that she could just leave and nothing would happen. Everything she did, every choice she made, everything she was—it was all a curse.

Chapter Seventeen

He felt like a complete jerk, but he had done the right thing by telling Shaye to leave. He picked up his phone and sent her another text message, hoping she would at least tell him that she had made it to the airport okay.

He had handled the whole thing terribly. But she wouldn't have left him unless she believed that he really didn't care. It was a lie he had to sell. And he had sold it well.

His message failed. Had she blocked him?

She was pissed. Actually, probably more than pissed. If he had been on the receiving end, he would have hated her.

That was it—she hated him.

And she had every right.

But he had to know she was at least safe.

He turned to Trevor. "I'm going to check on her."

Trevor nodded, then crossed his arms over his chest as he leaned against the wall outside the panic room. "Yeah, you probably should. You really hurt her, man."

He was more than aware. Not for the first time, he wished Trish was here. She would have told him what he should do.

And as he thought of Trish, he realized he was almost completely alone. Everyone he was capable of opening up to, everyone he could talk about his darkest secrets with, was gone.

"I screwed up." He had meant it with the best of intentions, but it was hard to live with the results.

"Nah," Trevor said, "you were right in wanting to get her out of here. The Gray Wolves are coming—maybe not right now, but they are coming…and they want us dead. You had to say what you had to say." He gave him a tired, drawn nod.

He was glad he had Trevor to talk to, and that his brother understood where he was coming from without a long, drawn-out conversation, but his approval did little to assuage the guilt he was feeling.

He hated lying.

He hated acting like the man Kash had made him out to be.

And, more than anything, he hated that

he had to watch her be hurt and then walk away—and he was the cause of her pain.

Even if he couldn't be the man in her life, or show her how much he loved her, he still needed to make sure she was okay. Though it seemed like the only way to get her to leave, he shouldn't have pushed her away like he had.

Damn it.

"I know you said you needed a break, but—"

"Go get her, make it right." Trevor waved him off. "Since she and the baby showed up you've started to get back to being yourself… And seriously, I love you, bro, but I don't think I can stand you sitting on the couch and eating Cheetos anymore."

"I do love Cheetos," he said with a laugh.

"And yet, even if I was blind, I could see that you love her more. Now, go get her." Trevor threw him his car keys and he stuffed them in his pocket.

Chad's heart lightened incrementally as he bounded up the stairs and, not bothering to even acknowledge his working family, ran out the door.

Shaye's rental car was still in the driveway, but Shaye was nowhere to be seen. Where had she gone? Had she gotten someone to pick her up?

Knowing her, she was probably hoofing it out of this place and just about ready to hitch-hike to anywhere but here.

No. She wasn't that careless.

But she had been in a hurry to get out of there.

He took out his phone and tried to call her, but the call didn't go through. *Stupid goddamn thing.*

He looked out on the porch, hoping to spot one of the guards that his sister had posted there, but they were gone. If he remembered correctly, Zoey had assigned men to the perimeter of their new enclosure and yet, he couldn't see a single guard. Lesson number one was always have a visible presence in scenarios like this one. He walked to the far side of the deck, where he would have stood if he had been tasked with acting as the family's sentinel.

There was a set of footprints in the snow from a man's boots.

On the railing, near the footprints, was a tiny speck of blood.

"Zoey!" he yelled, charging back toward the door in a mad dash to raise the alarm. "Zoey!" He pulled open the front door, making sure to close and lock it behind himself. "Did Shaye tell you where she was going?"

Zoey looked up from her tablet, looking somewhat annoyed that he had dared to pull her away from her work.

"You need to shut that stupid thing. I think we've got company," he said, pointing toward the front window, where someone had pulled the drapes closed.

"Huh? What?" Jarrod asked, getting to his feet. "What are you talking about?"

"How many men did you post outside?" Chad asked.

"Twenty-two. But there should be more on the way. If there was anything going on outside, I'm sure one of them would have reported something by now." Zoey set her tablet on the coffee table in front of her, but she kept looking back at the screen. "It's not like anyone could get the drop on us with that many feet on the ground."

"Not just anyone could, but a well-orchestrated group might be able to—a group like the Gray Wolves," Chad countered. "We know they've started to arrive, you've said as much. There's blood on our front porch and I don't see guards anywhere. And now Shaye…" His voice cracked, betraying his terror and panic. "Shaye is missing. I have to find her."

If something had happened to her because of what he had said, and if the Gray Wolves were behind it, he was going to personally kill every single man in their organization with his bare hands. And when he found Bayural, he would rip off his head and feed it to the crows.

He seethed with rage at the mere thought of Shaye being in harm's way.

She had to be okay. Maybe she had caught an Uber… Maybe the guard who was supposed to be on the porch had gotten a bloody nose or was taking a pee or something. Maybe he was just jumping to the worst-case scenario without cause.

And yet, he couldn't help the panic that rattled through him like he was an empty can without Shaye here.

He had to get her back.

But first he had to keep his wits about him. Shaye was fine. She was probably taking a walk. Maybe she was even thinking about how she was going to come inside and ream him out—she had every right.

Yeah, that was it. Shaye was just gearing up for a fight with him. Nothing more.

He let out a long exhale, attempting to quell his medley of negative thoughts.

Jarrod charged toward the window and barely pulled back the curtain to look outside. "She only beat you upstairs by a few minutes. She couldn't have gotten far," Jarrod said, taking in the steadily darkening world outside. "Zoey, can you pull up the cameras, see where she went?"

Zoey clicked to the cameras that were stationed in and around the house. Her screen turned black.

What in the actual hell?

He walked over, closer to the tablet, hoping he was just seeing things wrong or that he wasn't understanding something correctly.

But as Zoey clicked, the screen stayed black. She started hitting buttons faster and faster in a manic race for answers.

Jarrod turned away from the window and walked toward Mindy, who was still sitting on the couch.

Mindy looked up at him, a terrified look on her face. Jarrod put his hand on her shoulder as though he had the ability to calm her fears with just a touch.

Chad wished he had that kind of relationship with Shaye. Instead he had used her anger to manipulate her—even if he had thought it was for the greater good, he had made a mistake. He didn't deserve her. And once he found her, he would tell her exactly that and then drop down to his knees and kiss her feet and beg her forgiveness.

And he would tell her that he loved her.

Not that she would probably want to hear anything of the sort from him. She had to hate him right now.

"What is it, Zoey? What's going on?" Jarrod asked, almost as if Mindy had given him the strength to ask the question that everyone feared the answer to.

"Either there's something wrong with our connection or someone hacked our surveillance system," Zoey said, her voice strained and low. "I don't know how they could have done either. I built those firewalls myself, but something is wrong."

If she was panicking, then he should have been losing his freaking mind. And yet, Chad paused. He couldn't circle that drain. He had to take control.

"Zoey, work on getting those systems back up and running," he said. "In the meantime, Jarrod and the rest of the family will get suited up. We'll take post and make sure that no one enters the compound. I have to find Shaye."

"You can't go anywhere," Jarrod protested. "If we are under attack, you can't leave. The second you walk out those doors, you are going to have a target on your back."

"Well, then you'd better pull the trigger one second faster." He pulled out the Glock he always wore strapped to his ankle and made his way to the door.

He'd already gone out into the hot zone once and no one had fired on him. Maybe he'd been lucky, or maybe something else was going on. He had to be ready for whatever was going to come his way.

He slowly opened the front door. A man stood outside, an automatic weapon at rest in his hands and blood smeared down the side of his face. He wore a STEALTH jacket, marking him as one of their guards. He opened his mouth to talk and stepped forward, but he stumbled and fell into the house. His eyes rolled back in his head as he hit the floor with a loud thump. The gun dropped on the floor beside him with a clatter as the synthetic stock struck wood.

Grabbing him by the collar, Chad dragged him far enough inside that he could close the door. He took one more look outside but he couldn't see anyone.

"Hey, are you okay?" he asked, rolling the man over and checking his vitals.

There was a fast, erratic thumping under Chad's fingertips. The man was alive, but he was in pain.

Chad opened up his jacket. The guard was wearing a thick Kevlar vest—one of the older, standard-issue vests that some in their team still preferred in case of close-range impact.

At center mass were two copper slugs embedded in the fabric. He opened the jacket wider, but it stuck slightly as he pulled at the left side. There, he found a puddle of sticky blood. At the corner of his vest, near his armpit, the man had taken a hit.

The shock and sudden loss of blood must have sent him to the floor. He would be okay, as long as they got him some help.

He started to tend to the wound, staunching the bleeding as he yelled for someone to call for EMS. It would take twenty minutes for them to arrive, but the man would need more help than he could provide. Looking up, Zoey was already on the phone as he spoke. The world was whirling around him, fast and slow at the same time. He watched the man's chest rise and fall, but the voices around him all seemed to be muffled and all the words were being spoken at the same time, so nothing anyone said seemed to be audible.

"Hector," Zoey said, her voice finally breaking through the fog in Chad's head. "What happened?"

The man blinked, like he, too, was pulled back by her voice. "Gray Wolves. They ambushed us…" His voice was thin as he struggled to remain conscious.

"How many men do we have left?" Zoey asked.

Hector shook his head. "Lost radio contact—nothing is working. No phones. Nothing." Hector wheezed, the sound wet and rattling.

Chad wouldn't have been surprised if the man's lung had collapsed in his chest. They had to get him help.

"They must have bumped an electromagnetic pulse." Zoey balled her hands into tight fists. "The goddamn bastards. It's probably why everything stopped working."

Though he should have cared about the electromagnetic pulse that rendered their tech outside the Faraday-style walls of the house virtually dead, all he could think about was Shaye. "Did you see her? Is she okay?"

"Huh?" Hector asked, his eyes ablaze with pain.

"Shaye, did you see her leave?"

The man looked away from him, like he couldn't handle the shame. "She..."

"She what?" Chad's blood turned to thick syrup in his veins. He could have died from panic in those nanoseconds while he waited for Hector's answer.

"She was taken by the man who shot me." Hector coughed, blood spatter flecking his lips as he rolled on his uninjured side. "She is probably already dead. In the car." He pointed feebly toward the door.

No, his mind screamed. *No. She wasn't dead. The man was wrong. She was alive. He could feel her.*

"Her car?" Chad shot up to his feet.

Hector nodded.

He hadn't seen her when he had gone outside. There had been no movement. No sound. No sign of life.

He had nearly forgotten, but he was still holding his gun. It trembled in his hand as he looked down at the cold, black steel of its barrel. He wasn't sure if he was trembling out of terror or rage, or perhaps it could have even been merely adrenaline, but he had to get control. If he was going to walk out there—into what could have very well have been a shooting gallery—he was going to need every one of his faculties. He stuffed his handgun back into his ankle holster, clicking it in place.

He kneeled down by Hector and picked up the man's assault rifle. He checked the clip—it was nearly full. He grabbed the unused, full magazine clipped to Hector's utility belt.

Those bastards were going to pay.

Zoey touched his arm as he stood. "Find her, Chad. Find the woman you love. Save her if you can. We've got your back." She pulled her gun from her holster and stood up, every bit the badass he had always known his sister to be.

Trevor came up from the basement carrying assault rifles, always prepared, and he gave one to Jarrod. "You're not going out there alone—Martins stick together." He slammed a magazine into his gun and jacked a round into the chamber.

Together, they were unstoppable.

No matter how many Gray Wolves were out there, he and his family held the higher ground. If they were careful and did this right, they could pick off their enemies like they were prairie dogs.

Even Mindy, who normally stayed well out of the fray, took a gun. "I'll cover you guys." She moved beside the door.

He and Trevor got into formation, readying themselves to charge the door and make their way outside.

The odds were not in their favor to make it out of this.

Trevor gave him a grave look that told him that he knew what was at risk and was more than willing to do what needed to be done. Protection was a hard business, but there was nothing better than going out in a blaze of glory and honor.

If giving his life for hers was what he had to do, Chad would gladly make the sacrifice.

He gave Trevor a small nod. They would have to move fast but smooth. The old adage "slow is smooth, smooth is fast" came to mind.

Walking out into a possible active-shooter event was ballsy, and if Shaye wasn't out there, he wouldn't have risked it. Going outside and into the field of fire was setting them up for an ambush. But he had to do what needed to be done and be dynamic.

"Do you have a smoke grenade?" he asked, pointing at Trevor's utility belt.

Trevor answered with a wicked smile and pulled out the canister. There were two more on his belt and he tossed one to Chad, who stuffed it in his pocket. Trevor pulled the pin and chucked the smoke grenade out the door, letting the can land with a clang and roll. It exploded in a burst of light and green smoke.

Perfect.

He charged out the door and toward the car, using the smoke for coverage in the uncleared area.

He could hear the cracking and whizzing of shots fired and bullets striking the ground near him. But he didn't fire back.

No.

They needed all of the anonymity that the smoke could provide. If he shot recklessly now, they would only help their enemies pinpoint his location in the smoke. It was better to play the shadow.

Though the car was about twenty yards from the front door, it seemed like it was miles away. There was another barrage of shooting, but instead of instilling fear in him, it was like all of his senses came to life. He could smell the acrid smoke of the obscurant, and hear the crunch of the gravel and snow under his feet as he took steps toward the woman he loved. A bit of saliva collected in his mouth and he swallowed it back. Everything had to be under control. He gripped the gun tighter as he carefully held his ready position and stalked deeper into the smoke.

She was alive. She had to be alive. He repeated the words over and over to himself, trying to control his only real fear.

Trevor moved one step behind him, readying for anyone who approached from their nine or at their six. He could think of no better person to have at his side.

A bullet ripped through the air right in front of his face, so close that he could nearly make out the vortex the bullet had created in the smoke as it pierced the veil. He stopped for a moment, collecting himself. That single shot, two inches to the left, could've been the end of him.

He shook away the thought. Now wasn't the time to think about what-ifs. He would have plenty of time afterward.

Though it was not even above freezing outside, a tiny bit of sweat rolled down from his hairline over his temple, and he wiped it away.

He couldn't let the situation get out of hand, or get to him. He had spent thousands of hours training for this, but the only other operation that had felt like this was the day that Trish had died. The thought unnerved him.

No. Don't go there.

He took another step, calm and deliberate and in control. He was the master of his fate. And Shaye's life depended on him.

He moved forward until the magenta car came into view. Shaye was nowhere in sight. His stomach dropped. What if she wasn't out here? What if they had put themselves in danger for nothing?

Control. He had to remain controlled, deliberate.

He reached down and opened the driver-side door. Thankfully it was unlocked. Glancing inside, he could see Shaye lying in the back seat. She was hog-tied and there was black Gorilla tape over her mouth, its edges rolled slightly and her face reddened like she had been trying to rub off the tape.

That was his girl. Always the fighter.

As he looked in on her, she opened her eyes. He could see relief as she looked up.

"I'm here, babe. I've got you—you're safe now." He left the driver-side door open, hoping it would provide him an extra layer of protection from any rounds coming his way.

He motioned for Trevor to take cover in the car, as he stepped to the back door and opened it up. She tried to sit up, but the way she had been tied stopped any major movement.

Whoever had tied her up like this, whoever had done this to her, would pay. He pulled out a knife and cut the ropes at her wrists and ankles in two swift motions. She sat up and ripped the tape from her face with a tiny, pained squeak.

Aside from where the rope and tape had rubbed her skin raw, she looked no worse for the wear. At least whoever had taken her hadn't seemed to have done any physical harm. The simple courtesy may have just saved these men from dying a slow and painful death, but if Chad had his way they would still die.

"Mother hummer," she said, rubbing the place where the tape had taken off part of her skin. But she didn't let the pain slow her down. Instead, she looked at him. "I need a gun."

He handed her his handgun out of his ankle holster. "How many men are out there—do you know?"

"I just saw two, and it sounded like they were working for my father."

He frowned. They had come to believe that these men were all sent here by Bayural, and part of the Gray Wolves. Was her father somehow involved? Was he missing some vital clue? He felt like something was staring him right in the face, but yet he couldn't figure out what it was. And what did the woman and the child have to do with it all?

"But they were Gray Wolves, yes?" he asked.

She shrugged, making sure that there was a round in the chamber of the gun as she moved to step out of the car.

The wind kicked up and the smoke that hung in the air from the grenade started to dissipate. From where he stood, Chad could make out the outline of a man about ten yards to his right. He aimed at the man's center mass and fired twice. No hesitation, no regret.

The rounds struck and the man touched his chest where the bullet had entered as though surprised a bullet had found him. Shockingly, the man smiled. When he didn't drop to his knees, Chad realized he must have been wearing a vest.

Son of a...

Whoever was out there, they definitely weren't rookies. Their enemies knew what they were about. And this was one fight that would be hard-won. He pulled off another shot, this time taking an extra moment to carefully aim at the man's head.

His shot rang true. This time the man dropped.

One down. Who knew how many to go.

First things first—they needed better coverage than this car could provide.

He pulled the smoke grenade out from his

pocket and threw it in the direction of the house. It popped and a new cloud erupted into the air, providing them with a much-needed screen.

"Trevor, watch our six," Chad ordered.

Trevor answered with a simple nod. They moved together in a staggered line toward the safety the house and their family could provide.

It seemed even longer going back. The gunfire pinged around them, but thankfully the rounds seemed to be behind them as they moved. One lucky shot would be all it would take for them to ruin all of Chad's hopes and dreams.

He couldn't let Shaye get hurt. But at the same time, he couldn't simply put his arm over her and escort her through the smoke like she was some kind of victim. Shaye was never a victim. She had been through more than her fair share of crap in her life, but she would always be a strong, capable survivor. She was unflappable.

In fact, maybe if everything worked out, he could start training her for a role in STEALTH. They could always use another skilled team member.

As he spotted the front of the steps leading up toward the house, the gunfire around them exploded with a new wave of intensity.

Shaye squeaked from behind him, the noise almost like the one she had made when she had ripped the tape off her mouth. He stopped and turned. His gaze dropped to the ground near his feet. Shaye was down, clutching her abdomen with one hand and holding the gun with the other. She aimed to their right and started firing wildly, forcing Chad and Trevor to drop to the ground beside her.

"Are you okay?" he asked, reaching over to her and rolling her slightly so he could see what she was covering with her hands.

She looked up at him with wide eyes and a pained and terrified expression. Blood was seeping through her fingers as they were clamped to her belly.

Damn. Damn. Damn. He had done this to her. If only he would have kept his damn mouth shut...not pushed her away.

"You're going to be okay. Let me look at it," he ordered.

They only had a minute or so and then the smoke around them would start to thin and they would be at their enemy's mercy. He had to work fast to get her into the safety of the house or they would all be dead.

Trevor crawled to them. "We have to go!"

He didn't need to state the obvious.

Shaye wouldn't move her hands, so instead of forcing her to do anything she didn't feel comfortable doing, he leaned in. "I'm going to lift you, okay?"

She gave him a small nod.

Wrapping his arms around her, he lifted her up and got to his feet. She bit back a breath and he could feel her tense in his arms. Trevor covered them, sending out a spray of gunfire toward their enemies as they rushed up the steps and into the house, Mindy slamming the door behind them.

He would never forgive himself if she died. Hell, he was never going to forgive himself, period.

He ran to the couch and gently laid down Shaye. "She was hit," he said, his words sounding strangled.

"Watch out," Zoey said, moving to help her. She touched Shaye's hands, giving her a soft look. "It's going to be okay, Shaye. We have everything we need to keep you alive."

Shaye nodded, but there was fear in her eyes. When she looked at him, he wanted to tell her that he was sorry. That he had been wrong. That he'd been stupid. And yet, all he could do was smile at her.

"Shaye, no matter what happens, I want you to know I love you," he said, taking her hand.

Her eyes brimmed with tears. "I love you, too."

If he had the chance, he would spend the rest of his life apologizing, but for now all he could do was pray that she would come out of this alive.

Chapter Eighteen

There was a ping and crackle of glass as a bullet struck the front bay window. Shaye turned to look. Mindy stood beside the door, keeping guard. The window beside her had a circular hit, and a conical smattering of cracks where the round had hit—but not penetrated—what must have been bulletproof glass.

Zoey had done well picking this place.

It was strange for Shaye to be thinking about such things at a time like this, when she knew she had taken a bullet to the gut and was likely going to die a slow and painful death. Time had seemed to slow down. Every second was one she got to spend with the man holding her hand and standing at her side—the man who had told her that he loved her.

There were many things she had thought Chad would say to her when he had looked down on her, but confessing his love was the furthest thing from her mind. He had taken her by surprise, but she was glad he had said his piece.

If she was only going to live a few more hours or days, she wanted to spend her last moments with him. If that wasn't love, she didn't know what was.

Zoey gave her a soft, supplicating smile. "You're going to be okay, but I need to take a look at what you got going on here. Okay?"

She nodded, wanting to close her eyes and save herself the horror of seeing the hole in her belly and the blood dripping down her skin. It was already touch-and-go whether or not she would go into shock. But if she was going to go out, she was going to go out knowing what was in store for her.

Zoey lifted her black T-shirt gently, the fabric tugging on her skin as she pulled it up. Blood oozed from her stomach and as Zoey dabbed away the blood, a swollen black bruise was already rising on her skin. As Zoey inspected the wound, she smiled. "It's a flesh wound." Zoey looked up at her, her smile widening. "I bet you're glad you both took a break and put on the bulletproof gear."

Shaye inspected the wound. As she touched the bruised skin around the angry red circular mark, she winced with pain, but Zoey was right. She pulled the skin back a bit—there were definitely some lacerations, and she was going to be sore for a week or so, but she was going to be fine.

The bastards had failed to take her down.

She looked up at the normally calm and emotionally repressed Chad. Tears were streaming unchecked down his face. Though she didn't know whether they were from fear or relief, she didn't care. She was simply grateful that he was here, in her life, and they were together.

There was another ping and crackle as a second bullet struck the front window.

She pulled down her shirt and took in a pained breath as she moved to sitting. There was no way she could run around and fight without being in agony, but she wasn't going to be some broken woman that the Martins would have to treat like an invalid. She had to do her part to fight their enemies—enemies that she may well have brought to their gate. But first she needed to be there for the man who was here for her.

She got to her feet, wrapping her arms around Chad. "It's all okay. I'm fine," she said, gently hugging him. "Don't cry."

He rubbed the back of his hand over his cheeks, wiping away his tears even as others took their place. "I'm so sorry, Shaye. I shouldn't have—"

She silenced him with a finger to his lips. "I shouldn't have run off. If you love me like you say you do, make me a promise?"

He nodded.

"Please don't hurt me. I've already been hurt enough."

His tears moved faster and harder down his cheeks as he leaned in and took her lips with his, a promise sealed. It didn't matter to her that they were standing in front of his family or that there were active gunmen outside. In this short moment, all that mattered was he was giving her the world.

"Yes," he said, his breath against her lips. "But only if you make me a promise in return."

She nodded, no idea what he was going to ask of her, and it made her unexpectedly nervous.

"Shaye, if we get out of this alive, and it doesn't have to be right away or anything, but I want you to marry me. Sound like a plan?"

She couldn't help but laugh. "That is one a heck of a way to ask a girl to marry you. *Sound like a plan*," she said in a deep, mocking voice.

"I know it's not much of a way to ask a

princess for her hand, but you get what you see with me. I'm going to love you until the sun doesn't rise in the sky. No matter what comes, or doesn't come, I'm going to fight for you." He wrapped his arm tighter around her waist, drawing her closer against him.

She could have swooned in his arms, and for a moment the pain that was wracking her body disappeared.

"First, I'm far from a princess. And second, you and your proposal are absolutely perfect. I wouldn't change you for the world," she said, putting her hand on his chest just over his heart, which was beating wildly. "I want you with all your imperfections. I like to think our imperfections are what make us suited for each other."

"So we have a plan?" he asked with joy in his voice as the tears on his cheeks finally began to slow.

"Yes. A thousand times or a thousand ways or in a thousand languages, yes." The air left her lungs as he took her lips with his. The kiss was powerful and unrelenting as his tongue moved against her bottom lip. She met it with her own, tasting the bitterness of fear mixed with the sweetness of safety.

She, without a single regret or second

thought, whole-heartedly and without reservation, loved this man.

Trevor cleared his throat, pulling them both back to attention.

As wonderful as this was, and though she wanted to spend the rest of her life kissing those lips and feeling the warmth of his breath on her skin, their fight was far from over.

She pulled back from his arms, her body protesting the loss of his touch.

Her gun was sitting on the floor, its grip covered with her bloody fingerprints. Picking up the weapon, she knew exactly what she had to do.

"Get ready," she said, looking over her shoulder at the rest of the group and the wounded man that was resting on the other couch. "This is about to get crazy."

She moved toward the door, ready to take down all the men outside, but Chad gently took her by the arm, stopping her in mid-stride. "Soon-to-be Mrs. Martin, where do you think you're going?"

She nudged her chin in the direction of the door. "I'm about to go kill some dudes," she said, but even as the words came out she felt silly. This wasn't her. She was resilient and strong, but she had already fallen victim to their enemies once.

Chad gave her a serious look and shook his head. "I have absolutely no doubt that you could go out there and screw some people up, but we have to be smart about this. We can't go out guns blazing—you can see how well that worked the last time," he said, motioning to her stomach. "And no matter what, I'm not going to put you in a position in which you could get hurt. No way, no matter how badass you think you are."

Her back softened and she lowered the gun in her hands slightly. As she opened her mouth to speak, there was a low hum and then a familiar *thump, thump, thump*. The sound reminded her of a dog thumping its leg against the floor as it gave itself a good scratch.

She knew that sound, but she couldn't quite put her finger on what was making it.

Zoey rushed toward the window and looked up at the sky. A bullet pinged against the glass. "There's a helicopter."

Shaye ran over, hoping against all hope that it wasn't red and embellished with the Algerian flag.

No. He wouldn't have come this far for her.

He would send men, but he would never come himself.

A blue helicopter moved straight down, landing on the lawn near the driveway. She didn't recognize the man sitting behind the pilot, but her father sat on the other side of the stranger and beside him was the woman from the video—the woman who had dropped off the baby on their doorstep.

Holy shit… They were all working together.

The baby. Little Peanut. The woman had used a child to manipulate and slow them down. Who would have ever thought of using a child in such a brutal, compassionless way?

Those bastards.

Her father looked in Shaye's direction and their eyes met.

What was he doing here?

She was tempted to be relieved that her father was here. Perhaps she could negotiate some sort of treaty with him for both her and the Martins' safety. And yet she knew that her father would never go for such a thing. He was only there to snatch her and enslave her once again. No matter where she went, or whom she married, she would always be her father's slave. The only way she was going to get out from underneath his thumb would be either her death or his, and she preferred the latter.

"Who's that?" she asked, pointing at the man with her father.

Zoey glared at the man as Chad put his hand on Shaye's lower back and peered out the window.

"That is Fenrisulfr Bayural, the leader of the Gray Wolves." Chad's voice was thick with loathing. "He is the man responsible for Trish's death. I see he's made new allies."

A wave of sickness came over her as she stared at her father, the woman and Chad's enemy together. The leader of the Gray Wolves gave a malicious laugh, no doubt chuckling about how close they were to annihilating the people she loved… And maybe even her.

She stared out at Bayural. He had a wide face and an even wider nose and he reminded her a bit of a Turkish Benecio del Toro. He had the squished expression of a man who was on the verge of seeing his dreams come to fruition. Though there was little physical resemblance between him and her father— the same look of power and malice in their eyes that made them nearly twins.

Zoey hurried from the window and grabbed a house phone Shaye hadn't even noticed. It clinked against its cradle as Zoey lifted it and tapped on the numbers. She looked at them and then walked toward the kitchen.

"What is she doing?" Shaye asked, terrified at the prospect of losing more capable hands, hands that could make the difference in a firefight between life and death.

Chad shrugged. "I have no idea."

"What are we gonna do?" she said, lowering the gun until it brushed against the tops of her thighs. As she looked at Chad, she could tell that he was champing at the bit to get his hands on the man responsible for Trish's death. And yet, it wasn't feasible to leave the building. It was the only place they were guaranteed safety.

The man stepped out of the helicopter and readjusted the tie at his neck, almost as if he was going to business meeting and not here to put an end to an entire family. Her father and the woman remained in the chopper. Her father was no doubt hesitant to get his hands dirtied by coming within a foot of an active shooting situation.

She could make out the sounds of Zoey shouting what sounded like coordinates from within the kitchen.

But why?

Trevor stood beside Chad. "What do you think he's doing here?" he asked, motioning toward Bayural.

Chad shook his head. "Bayural has been chasing us for nearly a year. No doubt he knows he has us cornered and now he wants to watch the execution for himself. And Shaye's father… Well, he probably wants his daughter back." He reached down and took the gun from Shaye's hands. "But we're not going down without a fight."

She was glad to be free of the weight of the thing, but its absence made her feel vulnerable.

Zoey jogged out of the kitchen, the phone still in her hand. "Don't do anything. And get down!"

As she said the words, there was an ear-piercing boom from the skies above. And then a high-pitched whistle.

The world shuddered around them, and the roar of an explosion echoed through the room. She threw her arms over her head as she hit the floor. She heard the crash of glass and the scream of steel warping and bending against its will from the explosive power that had struck it.

No doubt, anyone outside the house and near the helicopter had been wiped out.

She dared to look out from underneath her arms. Chad was lying on the floor beside her, staring at her like a watchful partner. "You okay? How is your stomach? And your head?" He reached over and touched her temple, seemingly worried about the percussive force from the blast.

"I'm fine," she said, feeling like a broken record in her constant reassurance of her tenuous welfare.

The dust began to settle around them, coating Chad's dark hair with fine white powder.

After a moment, he got up and brushed himself off and offered her his hand. They walked to the window—the glass was missing and was lying on the floor, still in one piece but shattered. A fighter jet twisted in the skies overhead, celebrating their victory.

The rest of the family moved beside them as they looked out at the dusty scene in front of them. They held their guns at the ready, a show of power if she had ever seen one.

"Thank goodness for friends in high places," Zoey said, pointing at the sky with a satisfied smile.

"Who did you call?" Chad asked.

Zoey gave them a wide smile. "You're not the only one with an amazing fiancée. Sabrina has made a hell of a lot of friends in high places within the Pentagon. And as it turns out, the US government hated Bayural almost as much as we did. They were more than happy to use the coordinates we provided so they could take out such a high-value target."

Chad wrapped his arms around Shaye's body, pulling her into his embrace like he was her shield.

Shaye choked back the lump that had formed in her throat the moment she had seen her father. Where the helicopter had been, there was nothing more than a shallow pit. Scraps of burned metal and shrapnel littered the ground.

The cars that had been parked in the driveway were warped and blackened. The hood of her rental sat on the ground almost a hundred feet behind the car's body.

"I hope you got the insurance," Chad said, motioning toward her car.

She was glad he had said nothing of her father. She never wanted to talk or think about that despicable man again.

She couldn't help the dry laugh that escaped her. "I'll write them a check."

The family around her broke into stressed

laughter as they watched for any signs of movement outside, but the world around them remained as still as a grave.

Epilogue

The next day, snow had fallen on the ground, covering the mess that her father and Bayural had left in their stead. Though Shaye knew she should harbor some sort of grief for her late father, she felt only relief.

In fact, she had never been happier, especially when they left the cabin where her father had tracked them down.

Shaye sat on the couch, the sound of Christmas songs filling the air. Currently it was one of her lesser favorites—"Santa Claus Is Comin' to Town." It was nice, but she had always loved "Silent Night," even more so in the last few hours when all was calm and all was bright.

There was a knock on the front door. Chad walked over and opened it. Standing on the other side were Wyatt and Gwen, who was carrying the baby.

Thank goodness Chad had the foresight to

make sure the little one remained safe. She couldn't even bear to imagine what would have happened if they had kept the baby and put him in harm's way.

She already felt guilty enough as it was.

"Merry Christmas," Wyatt said, reaching beside the door and picking up a wreath he had propped against the door frame. He handed it over to Chad as they made their way inside. "We know you probably haven't even thought about the holidays with everything going on, but we wanted to invite you all over to celebrate with us at Dunrovin in the next few weeks."

"And we'd like all of you," Gwen added, looking over at Shaye, "and your significant others." She sent her a smile. "I hear that congratulations are in order."

Shaye blushed. "Yes, I'm going to use my mother's ring. The one her mother gave her."

"That's perfect," Gwen said, her smile growing impossibly larger.

"I'm having it resized but I'll have to show it to you when I get it back—it should be here before Christmas. It's beautiful. It's a Harry Winston with a platinum band and a diamond at its center."

"I'm sure it's breathtaking," Gwen said, readjusting the baby high on her hip. "And

I take it that you will be coming for Christmas then?"

"We'd love to," Chad said, looking around at his brothers and Zoey as they nodded in agreement.

"Anything we can bring?" Trevor asked.

"Just yourselves, and that ring," Gwen said, giving her a private wink. "Mrs. Fitzgerald always goes over the top. Be prepared for lots of bows and wrapping paper. Oh, and that tree, at night when the light hits the gold…" Gwen sighed as the baby squirmed in her arms.

Shaye walked over and lifted back the hood on the baby's coat—a coat he hadn't had when they had given the boy to Wyatt. He smiled, but tucked his body in the safety of Gwen's body. "What a happy boy. Thank you so much for taking him," Shaye said, making funny faces at the baby, who giggled as she made googly eyes.

"It was our pleasure," Gwen said, walking into the living room and setting down a brand-new diaper bag on the floor.

"Oh, hey…we have a diaper bag the woman dropped off." Shaye snapped her fingers as she remembered the boy's diaper bag.

As she went to grab it, Wyatt turned to Chad. "About the men you'd been keeping as hostages—we have locked them up and charged them with obstruction of justice, attempted homicide and a litany of other things. They shouldn't be seeing anything but cell bars for the rest of their lives."

Shaye let out a breath she hadn't known she was holding. Glancing back at the family, she took in the sight of them all together— one unit, one powerful force.

"And as for the event that occurred at the cabin last night," Wyatt continued, "news sources are calling it a gas explosion. It was lucky you all weren't there," he said, giving them all a look that spoke of his lie—a lie he provided in order to protect his family. "However, there were some out-of-towners who were killed…looks like it was a hideout of some sort for a terrorist group out of Turkey. Who knew, am I right?" Wyatt looked over at her and gave her an apologetic nod. "And there were also reports that there was a foreign dignitary, a guy from Algeria, on site. They are saying that he was involved in some manner of corruption."

"I have to say, it's always a positive when corrupt officials are taken care of," Zoey said, giving him a salty smile. "Thank you, Wyatt. I know this wasn't an easy mess to clean up—or an easy choice to make to help us."

"After you filled me in on the truth, making the choice to help my extended family wasn't hard at all—it was the right thing to do. However, what *was* messy was trying to explain away a military jet flyover." He smirked. "We even got reports that there were UFOs or bombs. There was all kind of crazy talk." He waved it off.

Shaye grabbed the bag that sat at the top of the stairs and took it into the living room. Opening it up, she pulled out its contents. "We have some diapers, a few clothes and an empty bottle." She turned over the diaper bag and dumped everything out so they could take a quick inventory.

However, as she gripped the bag, her fingers pressed against something hard and lumpy on the bottom of the bag. She let go to reveal a patch. It blended almost seamlessly with the bag, but as Shaye picked and pulled at the stitches at its edges, the patch gave way. She pulled off the patch and there, sitting on the bottom of the bag, was a small black plastic thing that looked a bit like a thumb drive. "What is this?"

Zoey walked over and took it out of her hand. She lifted it up, squinting as she tried to read something that was inscribed on the plastic. "Holy...they used our own gear against us. Bayural was one son of a…" Zoey looked at the baby and stopped before swearing. "This is one of our GPS trackers. We have them implanted in the guns that we sell to terrorist groups. It's how we were supposed to find the Gray Wolves. Not the other way around." She paused. "Those bastards used the baby like a goddamn Trojan Horse. And that goddamn woman…she never deserved to be a mother. At least he has us now, and a family who will love him." Zoey's voice cracked with emotion.

Zoey was right. Some people didn't deserve to have children. Children were meant to be loved, cherished and protected—not thrown into the middle of a war zone.

Shaye shook her head as she stared at the tracker.

A thought sprang to the front of her mind and she tried hard to control her smile. She hadn't been the one to bring their enemies upon them. She had merely been a part of a giant puzzle. Chad wrapped his arms around her waist and hugged her against his body.

"I told you so," he whispered into her ear. "I told you that none of this was your fault."

She smiled up at him and bumped against him with her butt playfully. "I'm relieved.

But has anyone ever told you that no one ever likes to hear 'I told you so'?"

One of his eyebrows shot up. "Well, hello, Ms. Snark."

She giggled. "No, you pronounce it Mrs. Martin."

Chad laughed, the sound throaty and rich. He leaned down and gave her a soft kiss on her neck.

Wyatt cleared his throat. "Speaking of children, the baby was part of the reason we wanted to come here today. If you are okay with it, we were hoping that we could adopt him."

"You want to adopt Peanut?" Chad asked, surprised.

Wyatt nodded. "And actually, we've started calling him Peter for short."

Chad chuckled. "You gave him a *real* name. I like it." He turned to face her. "This sounds like a good idea to me—what do you think?"

Her heart lurched in her chest. Though she wanted nothing more than to take the baby and give him a home, she wasn't in a position to provide for him as well as Gwen and Wyatt. They were married, had a home, family, stability. So much had happened in her life recently that Shaye held no doubt that she would need time to get herself back in order…even with Chad's help.

She nodded through the pain. "I think it would be best. But I would love to be Peter's auntie, and Chad his uncle."

Chad walked over and put his hand in hers. He lifted their entwined hands and gave hers a soft, loving kiss. He must have known how hard the choice was, and from the pained but happy expression on his features, he was feeling the same.

But they had to do what was best for the baby.

Love was sacrifice, and true love was agony.

It was agony that had brought them together. Agony and grief had cemented their friendship, which then became something so wonderful that for years to come, each time she looked over at him, he would take her breath away.

* * * * *

Get 4 FREE REWARDS!

We'll send you 2 FREE Books plus 2 FREE Mystery Gifts.

Harlequin Romantic Suspense books are heart-racing page-turners with unexpected plot twists and irresistible chemistry that will keep you guessing to the very end.

FREE
Value Over
$20

YES! Please send me 2 FREE Harlequin Romantic Suspense novels and my 2 FREE gifts (gifts are worth about $10 retail). After receiving them, if I don't wish to receive any more books, I can return the shipping statement marked "cancel." If I don't cancel, I will receive 4 brand-new novels every month and be billed just $4.99 per book in the U.S. or $5.74 per book in Canada. That's a savings of at least 13% off the cover price! It's quite a bargain! Shipping and handling is just 50¢ per book in the U.S. and $1.25 per book in Canada.* I understand that accepting the 2 free books and gifts places me under no obligation to buy anything. I can always return a shipment and cancel at any time. The free books and gifts are mine to keep no matter what I decide.

240/340 HDN GNMZ

Name (please print)

Address   Apt. #

City   State/Province   Zip/Postal Code

Mail to the **Reader Service:**
IN U.S.A.: P.O. Box 1341, Buffalo, NY 14240-8531
IN CANADA: P.O. Box 603, Fort Erie, Ontario L2A 5X3

Want to try 2 free books from another series? Call 1-800-873-8635 or visit www.ReaderService.com.

---

*Terms and prices subject to change without notice. Prices do not include sales taxes, which will be charged (if applicable) based on your state or country of residence. Canadian residents will be charged applicable taxes. Offer not valid in Quebec. This offer is limited to one order per household. Books received may not be as shown. Not valid for current subscribers to Harlequin Romantic Suspense books. All orders subject to approval. Credit or debit balances in a customer's account(s) may be offset by any other outstanding balance owed by or to the customer. Please allow 4 to 6 weeks for delivery. Offer available while quantities last.

Your Privacy—The Reader Service is committed to protecting your privacy. Our Privacy Policy is available online at www.ReaderService.com or upon request from the Reader Service. We make a portion of our mailing list available to reputable third parties that offer products we believe may interest you. If you prefer that we not exchange your name with third parties, or if you wish to clarify or modify your communication preferences, please visit us at www.ReaderService.com/consumerschoice or write to us at Reader Service Preference Service, P.O. Box 9062, Buffalo, NY 14240-9062. Include your complete name and address.

HRS20R

Get 4 FREE REWARDS!

We'll send you 2 FREE Books plus 2 FREE Mystery Gifts.

PRESENTS

Indian Prince's Hidden Son

USA TODAY BESTSELLING AUTHOR
LYNNE GRAHAM

PRESENTS

The Greek's One-Night Heir

USA TODAY BESTSELLING AUTHOR
NATALIE ANDERSON

Harlequin Presents books feature the glamorous lives of royals and billionaires in a world of exotic locations, where passion knows no bounds.

FREE
Value Over
$20

COMING NEXT MONTH FROM

⊕HARLEQUIN

INTRIGUE

Available March 17, 2020

1917 48 HOUR LOCKDOWN
Tactical Crime Division • by Carla Cassidy

When TCD special agent and hostage negotiator Evan Duran learns his ex, Annalise Taylor, and her students are being held hostage, he immediately rushes to the scene. They'll need to work together in order to keep everyone safe, but can they resolve the situation before it escalates further?

1918 LEFT TO DIE
Badge of Honor Mystery • by Rita Herron

When Jane Doe finds herself stranded in a shelter during a blizzard, all she knows is that she has suffered a head injury and ranger Fletch Maverick saved her. Can they discover the truth about Jane's past before an unseen enemy returns to finish what he started?

1919 WHAT SHE DID
Rushing Creek Crime Spree • by Barb Han

Someone is terrorizing Chelsea McGregor and her daughter, and Texas rancher Nate Kent is the only person who can help Chelsea figure out who is after her. But can she trust an outsider to keep her family safe?

1920 COVERT COMPLICATION
A Badlands Cops Novel • by Nicole Helm

Gina Oaks tried to forget Agent Cody Wyatt, but her old feelings come flooding back the moment she sees his face again. Now she's in danger—and so is Cody's daughter. He'll do anything to protect them both, even if that means confronting the most dangerous men in the Badlands.

1921 HOSTILE PURSUIT
A Hard Core Justice Thriller • by Juno Rushdan

In twenty-four hours, marshal Nick McKenna's informant, Lori Carpenter, will testify against a powerful drug cartel. Nick has kept her safe for an entire year, but now, with a team of cold-blooded assassins closing in, he'll have to put it all on the line for his irresistible witness.

1922 TARGET ON HER BACK
by Julie Miller

After discovering her boss has been murdered, Professor Gigi Brennan becomes the killer's next target. Her best chance at survival is Detective Hudson Kramer. Together, can they figure out who's terrorizing her...before their dreams of a shared future are over before they've even begun?

ReaderService.com has a new look!

We have refreshed our website and
we want to share our new look with you.
Head over to ReaderService.com
and check it out!

On ReaderService.com, you can:

- Try 2 free books from any series
- Access risk-free special offers
- View your account history & manage payments
- Browse the latest Bonus Bucks catalog

RS19